ERIK'S END

THE O-LINE SERIES BOOK 5

Kidnapped as a child and raised within an Ohio-based Russian mafia post, Erik Pavel has been honed to a razor's edge—ruthless and deadly. Yet, at age fifteen, the head of his brigade deems Erik weak and murders his surrogate mother, fueling him to live for only one thing—revenge. Now closer than ever to the vengeance he seeks, Erik will allow no one to stand in his way.

Nicki Nobles fought her way out of a life where survival was key. Now strong and independent, she refuses to let her past dictate her future.

After Nicki helps him gather information on his nemesis, Erik is forced to work with her again. Fearing for her safety while fighting an attraction to her, Erik would prefer to keep Nicki out of his life.

Seeing so much of herself in the broken man, Nicki agrees to Erik's plan only to discover she's falling for someone who will never believe she can be more than her past.

As Erik's plan unfolds, he must learn to rely on Nicki and realize that families aren't always bound by blood and that trusting another doesn't make you weak.

ERIK'S END

THE O-LINE SERIES

JILLIAN JACOBS

JILLIANJACOBS.COM

CHAPTER ONE

Nightmares weren't supposed to occur during the day. Wasn't that a rule somewhere? So, why was this vision occurring right before her eyes? Couldn't she enjoy her lunch in peace? Apparently not since this unwelcome blast from her past just strolled through the door like he owned the joint.

Leaning against the door leading into her esthetic services and message therapy treatment room, Nicki Nobles licked the cheese curl's orange powder off her fingers. Though feigning nonchalance, she was very aware that any sudden moves might cause the predator stalking toward her to strike.

Otari Korzakov grinned at Nicki's co-workers as he strode through the Beauty Bar and Spa followed by his henchman, Yegor.

Yegor looked like a pro-football team's linebacker if Chernobyl had a team. The Russian could certainly tackle, a fact she'd learned the hard way. A towering monstrosity at six-six, with an off-kilter nose and acne scars along his jawline. His brown hair was cut military style, and he stared at her with soulless brown eyes.

Nicki could run. Flee the building, but her next appointment was set to arrive. And this *was* a public place *and* she no longer cowered.

Never again would Korzakov buy her body for the night because her days as a high-dollar escort were over. Yet the memories of the times he'd struck her made her eye twitch. She'd hit back as good as she'd got, because hadn't she always fought? Hadn't she learned at a young age that pleasure and pain were one and the same? And Korzakov was a master at delivering pain. One night he'd shown her just how dark he could be.

She held back a shiver as he met her gaze across the bustling salon. The pungent blend of chemicals burned through her nose. A local radio station's commercial shouted a used car sale through the overhead speakers. Everyday normal sounds and scents, yet...couldn't the stylists smell his evil? Couldn't they see past his high-dollar beige suit and ostentatious gold Rolex and glimpse the monster within?

Korzakov crossed the room, indicating with a jerk of his head for his lap dog, Yegor to go to the front door.

Nicki crumpled the half-empty snack bag of cheese curls in her hand and tossed what was left of her lunch into the garbage bin. Widening her stance, she crossed her arms over her chest and arched a brow at Korzakov. "What do you want?"

"Careful how you speak to an old friend."

His voice was soft, almost feminine. It matched his petite stature. But what he lacked in stance, he made up for in bite. He hadn't changed—still fastidious, standing at around 5'6", dyed brown-blond hair, and blue eyes. She'd always likened him to a well-dressed troll, big nose and big ears included.

Nicki considered the distance to the back door. Five steps. Seven? Though Korzie likely had a minion waiting around back ready to toss her into a SUV with black-tinted windows. Torture and mayhem would likely ensue so she stayed put—for now. "I have an appointment coming." She grabbed a heated damp towel from the manicurist's cabinet and wiped the leftover powder from her fingers.

"I *am* your appointment."

"No, thank you." She flipped her straight, dark brown hair over her shoulder, because, *bitch, please and no thank you.* Maybe she should run, but in her heels, she'd probably trip and fall.

"You think to refuse me?" Brow lifted, Korzakov trailed his thumb across his upper lip before tapping it against his chin.

"Uh, yes." She flashed a fake grin and tossed the orange-stained towel in the laundry bin outside her door. "As a matter of fact, I'd like you to leave."

When he came to the club, he'd always picked her, because she fought back. Then one night she'd knocked him out, and he'd come back with Yegor and Georgy. They'd held her down, each man taking a turn, and that hadn't even been the worst thing he'd done that night. She shook off the unwelcome memories.

"You wound me." He placed a hand against his chest.

She narrowed her eyes. "I doubt that."

"Such a hard one now...when you used to be so...soft." Slinking forward, he ran a finger along her arm.

Jaw clenched, she edged two steps toward the back door. Perhaps, she should scream for everyone to leave the building. She swallowed hard and pulled her phone from her front pocket, thinking to call someone, because this man was pain-personified. Yet, who could she call? He owned a lot of cops in town. She'd watched him entertain them at his club. Maybe she'd send a distress signal to someone more versed in Russian mafia tactics like, Erik Pavel? *Uh, hell no. Bad thought.* Erik was *not* anyone's hero. His dark hair and dark eyes matched his dark heart.

Plus, she could do this. She was a businesswoman, and she didn't have to take Korzakov's shit anymore. She lifted her chin. "What can I do for you?"

"As I said, I have an appointment for a full-body massage."

No. Nope. "I don't believe you. Everything you do has an angle. A reason." And her fingers were *not* touching his wrinkled ass ever again. "I'll ask again, what do you want?"

He grabbed her elbow and forced her into the room.

Oh shit. How could everything she'd fought to become—her hope that she was a strong, independent woman—be erased by a man who'd used her in the cruelest way possible? A man who'd ripped her body apart with brute force. And a man, who'd, murdered a bloody and broken child on that same horrific night. At times, she'd wake from nightmares of that little girl's glassy eyes. The bullet hole, dripping blood from her forehead, and the worst thought of all, was that Nicki sometimes believed the tiny redhead was better off dead. No one should have to carry around that kind of pain, and yet, Nicki did every day.

Erik Pavel wasn't the only person on this Earth who wanted a random satellite to land on Korzakov's head. Maybe Yegor would be close by and they'd both die. *Where was karma when you needed her?*

Korzakov stopped just inside her door, shut it, and then spun her around. "I know of your friendship with Pavel."

Nicki kept her expression blank, but her mind pictured her foot far up Erik's ass. Of course everything led back to him—and just when she'd started to move on from whatever she'd felt for the asshole. *Foolish stupid, heart!*

"I do not know the extent of your friendship with Pavel, but I am extending an offer of *my* friendship instead. You and I were partners before. I see no reason we cannot reach another agreement."

Weren't Korzakov's words so pretty, when his heart was so black? She cursed her deep V-necked black knit dress, which revealed too much to this vile man. "I'm through with that life. Through with you."

He glanced around the room before arching a brow. "Are you?"

"Yes." Fuck him for obviously finding her life lacking. She clenched her hands into fists but buried under her arms.

Shifting away, he lifted the lid on her wax jar then sniffed the contents. "Then Pavel is...what to you?"

"Can you not fiddle with my stuff?" Nicki put a hand on the doorknob, briefly wondering if Yegor had meandered to the other side in case she decided to bolt. "Pavel was simply a means to an end."

She shrugged and hoped he bought her nonchalance. "I got my end. That's all."

"I also seek a means to an end." He leaned against her massage bed and met her gaze.

An end to what? Did he plan to kill Erik? And why did that thought make her heart burn in her chest? She and Erik had worked together for about six months, finished, and then moved on. She wanted nothing to do with a man who only had revenge in his heart. No matter if said man made her care just a little. Why was she continually falling for hopeless cases?

She faced Korzakov, hoping he wouldn't shoot her on the spot for turning him down. "Don't look to me for help. I'm not interested in what you term an 'end.'" Nicki crooked her fingers into air quotes. "An *end* in your part of the world means death, so...no thank you. Been there, seen that, and I have the nightmares to prove it. So...now, if that's all, please, go."

"Ah...but I so enjoyed our...ends." With a lecherous grin, he trailed his gaze over her body. "You were always so beautiful in that moment of ecstasy. I've missed you and everything we did together."

Swallowing the bile from the memories flashing through her mind, she closed her eyes and rubbed her eye sockets. *Don't go back there. Just don't.*

With men like Korzakov, everything boiled down to what they owned. He had no trouble wielding her past like a knife, and cut he did. She clenched her jaw. If she had to stand for every woman he'd ever used, then that is where she'd find her strength. Taking a deep breath, she met his gaze. "I was *paid* to be with you. I let you beat me so you could get off. I'm not interested in any sort of arrangement with you or any man, and, to be honest, any woman either. So, get the hell out of my room and don't come back."

He laughed while clapping his hands together. "You always were one for dramatic speeches." He stepped closer and trailed a finger along her jaw. "Salty and sweet, my favorite kind of dish."

"I'm not sweet." Nicki jerked away.

"But you are. I remember every bit of your taste. I remember you down on your knees. I remember sliding inside that slick and ready body. I owned you once. You think you've become a career girl, but you'll always be that whore looking for your next trick."

"Enough." Nicki slapped him across the face with such force that her hand stung, but she reveled in the pain. *Damn it.* She no longer lost control like this. She jabbed a finger at the door. "Get out and don't come back."

Placing a palm against his bright red jaw, he grinned. "I like when you hiss and spit. You know I like it rough, and so do you. Don't test me, or I'll make sure it's really rough. You remember that night, right?" He adjusted his cock. "Think over my offer."

Averting her gaze from his obviously aroused-oh-so-gross dick, Nicki stared down at the man. Height sometimes had its advantages. "What offer am I supposed to think over? I'm not an escort anymore, and I sure as hell won't partner with you on any scheme against Erik." Had she just shouted? Her coworkers were just starting to accept her. What would they think if they heard her words?

"This is my offer, so listen." Korzakov gripped her forearm and squeezed.

And now his real colors came out. *Fantastic.*

"You will stick by Pavel's side and discover his plans."

"No, I won't." Mostly because Erik Pavel was basically a sociopath, living for revenge and no woman could ever redeem him. After spending time with him, she'd wanted to try, which was completely ridiculous and cliché and everything else she'd already said to herself a zillion times.

"I don't believe I phrased my offer as a question." Korzakov glared and tightened his hold on her arm. "Now, you will call when you have information." With his free hand, he produced a card from his suit jackets pocket. "Here's my card."

She took the card, ripped it in half, and tossed it back in his face.

"Oh, that was unnecessary." He pulled another from his jacket, and then, as quick as a snake, he had his hand at her throat. "Don't test me again."

"Go play evil villain with someone else. I'm over your shit."

"You have no say in this matter." He loosened his hold on her neck, but pressed his hard cock against her thigh.

"Don't I?" Nicki met his gaze, because once again this man had pressed his disgusting puny erection upon her and that was unacceptable. "The way I see this story going is I go to Erik and tell him about your visit. Apparently, you're afraid of him. I don't blame you. He's one cold-ass motherfucker. And *you* killed his mother. He's younger, stronger, and smarter than you. If I was on anyone's side, it'd be his."

"Big mistake."

She arched a brow. She was finished talking and wouldn't win an argument anyway, because Korzakov was a monster. "Bah-bye now." She fluttered her fingers in the air between them.

Korzakov shoved his card between her cleavage, opened her door, and left.

Nicki took a deep breath, closed and locked her door, then dropped to the floor. Fury and fear warred within her. This was all Erik Pavel's fault.

And Ariel's.

Ariel—a woman from her past and the only person Nicki had ever loved—both literally and figuratively, had betrayed her. As a result, Nicki spent two years in jail for crimes she hadn't committed but instead had been elaborately developed by her lover.

Once Nicki's prison sentence was complete, she'd returned to Ohio to seek revenge. After discovering Ariel was attempting to trap a rich man, Nicki recruited Erik. In return, she provided him with information on Korzakov's habits. Together they'd stopped Ariel before she ruined another person's life. Done with that project, she and Erik no longer needed to continue their relationship.

The sad truth was, at the end of their alliance, Nicki had taken a chance and offered to help him destroy Korzakov's empire. She'd asked for a continued partnership, and in doing so, the implication had also been, she'd open her heart.

He'd laughed in her face and told her they were finished. She'd served her purpose, and he would never completely trust a woman who'd been in Korzakov's bed. With those harsh words, he'd severed everything.

But Korzakov had just brought the fight back to her door. She never should have walked away from Erik. He needed help destroying the Russian mafia menace. Hadn't today's visit proved that her past would keep creeping back until the man was scorched from the earth? So she'd try again with Mr. Erik Pavel—but this time, she'd leave her heart out of it.

CHAPTER TWO

Blinking awake, Erik Pavel fumbled for his beeping cell phone. Someone was pounding on his door. Not many people knew where he lived, so this visit was rare—and likely unwelcome. Grabbing his .45 out of his headboard's cubby, he checked his phone's outer security camera app and saw Nicki Nobles standing with her arms crossed and her toe tapping just outside his door—at one a.m.

He should just ignore her.

He'd done it before.

But...damn it!

Nicki Nobles. The dark-haired, green-eyed beauty with a wicked body and plush lips he'd like to destroy with his own was outside his door in the middle of the night. Why? Their business was through. He'd made sure of it. He'd walked away because things had become... intense, for lack of a better word. He didn't have time for, nor did he want, *intense.*

She'd made him shift focus. He'd made excuses to spend time with her. Who did that? Not him. Not now. Not ever. Plus, by merely being in his presence, she was in danger. And she'd been through enough in her short life, even though technically she was three years older than his twenty-three.

Wait a second, how did he even *know* her age? Seemed like he was unsure of a lot lately and that raised all sorts of red flags. Especially when his reckoning with Korzakov was so close he could smell the blood in the water. The sharks were circling, and soon his mother's killer would learn bigger predators ruled the sea.

After tossing his gun back on his rumpled bed and throwing on a pair of sweatpants, he flipped on lights while stumbling down the hallway. "Gah." He squinted against the glare and held a hand over his eyes, trying to block the blasting light. Deep sleep rarely came easy to him so this interruption after he'd finally dozed was not welcome.

The pounding continued.

"Just a minute." Erik shouted toward the door. "Jesus. Calm down, Nicki." He ripped open the door, grabbed her arm, checked the perimeter, and then yanked her inside.

"What the hell, Pavel?" Nicki glared over her shoulder, struggling to break free.

He tried not to notice her soft skin or that familiar bubble gum scent, which came from her constantly chewing the shit. Why hadn't her teeth rotted out of her mouth by now? After giving her arm a warning squeeze, he reluctantly let her go. "What the hell, *Pavel?* You're the one banging down *my* door. What are you doing here?" He crossed both arms over his chest then frowned as she made her way to the kitchen as if she had every right to claim what was his.

She opened the fridge and grabbed one of the beers he'd purchased tonight from a local brewery. "I've spent the entire drive over here waging a mental argument with myself. Common sense didn't win. Imagine that. So, here's the thing." She opened the bottle and took a long drink.

Lifting a brow, he leaned against the kitchen archway. The white space seemed so plain against her vibrancy. That smooth, perfect skin. Those bright pink lips and her glittering green eyes.

"What are you looking at?" Hip cocked, she glanced down at herself as if looking for a bug or stain on her shirt.

He rolled his eyes, fighting down his very visceral response to her playing the drama queen. Nicki Nobles was all swish-swish, I'll-cut-you-bitch, which he admired in a woman. And in her tight dark jeans, and almost threadbare Manchester Marauders T-shirt, he found *a lot* to admire.

"Korzakov came to see me today and—"

"Whoa!" Erik held up a hand, and his asset-admiration skidded to an abrupt halt. He stormed forward and glared down at her. "He what?"

"Just shut up a second." She flicked a hand in the air. "I have a whole speech planned and you're ruining it."

No one spoke to him that way. No one. So why was he letting her? Maybe the drama thing. Her tirades always made her skin all flush, which made *him* hot as fuck.

And another red flag shot up in his mind. *Shut her down. Now.* One way to do that would be to bite that plump bottom lip and—

"...he wanted me to spy on you."

"What?" He shook his head, refocusing because he'd missed a lot staring at her lush mouth.

"Why do you keep saying *what*? I said I had a speech planned and you saying *what* is only stalling things, so pay attention." She jabbed his forehead with an index finger.

He grabbed her finger and pulled her close. "Don't, 'cause I bite."

"I already asked you to bite me." She flashed a grin then hovered with her lips just inches from his. "But you said no."

Before he lost himself in her bubble-gum-flavored mouth, he stepped back and shook his head. "Okay, what—"

"Do you remember the movie, *Pulp Fiction*? Do you know what happened to the kid who said *what* one more time?"

"Wh—" Erik banged his fisted hand against the stainless-steel fridge. "I have no idea wh...I mean, go back...Korzakov came by to visit. Start there, please."

She sipped her beer, her pinky finger sticking up in the air before she placed the bottle on the white marble countertop and huffed out a long sigh.

Drama. Queen.

"Korzakov came by the Beauty Bar today and asked me to spy on you. He thinks he can bully people. Thinks he owns me. Thinks just because he paid to...to...you know...he thinks he can control me." She shoved Erik aside and paced in front of his stove. "But no. Never again. Each time, he took a piece of me, and even though I thought I'd buried that part of my past, I can't because I'm meant...I'm supposed to *do* something. How many girls like me are out there? How many work for Korzakov? So many girls are struggling to survive, using the only thing they have...their bodies." She stopped and turned to Erik. "You and I were a team, and I want that again. I won't make the mistake of asking you for anything more. I know your limitations, but can't you maybe just once entertain the notion that you were meant for something bigger, too? That together, with everything we've been through, maybe we can turn all that nasty...just misery from our pasts into something that could help those who are suffering as we did?"

"Are you finished?" Even though her words came from her heart, he could not and would not let her move him. He lived his life striving for one goal. Her dream to make the world a better place meant nothing, and her attempts to dig some sort of humanity from him only made him want to cut her deeper. How dare she come here and *once again* beg him for something he didn't know how to give. He lifted his head and met her gaze, hoping she'd see nothing but cold ruthlessness.

"Don't level that supercilious gaze on me, Pavel."

"Look who's been playing with the dictionary app again."

"You are a dick." She spaced out each word for maximum effect. "Don't need an app to come up with that."

Speaking of dicks, his was hard, its usual state in her presence. He wanted her. Forbidden fruit and all that—but maybe, the real truth was that out of every person he'd ever known, Nicki Nobles could understand who and what he was.

But, he couldn't get past the fact she'd been in bed with his enemy. He hated that he saw her—this beautiful, strong woman—as nothing but Otari Korzakov's cast off. She deserved more, and yet he couldn't give her more. In fact, he wasn't any better than Otari. He wanted her body. Her passion. Just looking at her now—her bright eyes, flushed skin, her total involvement in the moment—he knew she'd be his match in bed. They'd fuck for days, but he had plans that would never involve her. His life wasn't open to a woman capable of making him feel anger, lust, and total exasperation. She'd make him weak and vulnerable. Otari was already trying to use her against him. She'd end up lying on the floor, her hair across her face, and a bullet in her chest.

That vision hardened his resolve. "I told you before, I got what I needed from you. And, in return, you were in a position to spy on Ariel." He scrubbed a hand across his bare chest before raking his fingers through his sleep-disheveled hair. "Our arrangement ended."

"But it doesn't have to." Voice, slightly husky, Nicki clutched his bicep. "I want to help you bring down Korzakov. Can't you see I *know* your world. I can help."

"You did help." Erik shook her off. "I don't need you anymore."

"Well, I don't *need* you either." She rolled her eyes and dropped his arm as if it were germ-infested. "I can pursue the monster on my own. I would think you'd appreciate my offer though, especially since your mother's story is so similar to my own."

Erik shoved a finger in Nicki's face. "Don't you dare bring her into this. Your manipulations won't work on me. You forget I learned from a master."

"Exactly, and how many more people, like you, like me, like your mom, have to learn from someone like your stand-in father, Victor Pavel or Otari Korzakov?" Gazing down, she ran a finger along the rim of her beer bottle. "Ariel didn't make me who I am today. She betrayed me, sure, but men shaped me. From the very beginning my body wasn't my own. I was used, torn up, and discarded. I was a vessel. I've risen above that, so shouldn't I help others do the same?"

"No."

"No?" She lifted her head and peered into his eyes.

"You don't owe anyone anything." Erik shook his head. *What a naïve fool.*

"I can't stand idle. I-I just can't."

"Volunteer at a half-way house or something then." He raked a hand through his hair again before glancing at the time on his microwave. Maybe she'd take the hint and leave. "Listen, it's late and—"

"I'm gonna be on the front line." She finished her beer and tossed the bottle into the recycling bin.

"Well, don't look for me to stand beside you. I haven't got time for your save-the-world campaign, and, to be blunt, I don't care about you *or* your ridiculous causes."

"That's a lie."

"No, that's fact." He grabbed a beer out of the fridge, because he either gripped the cold bottle, or he gripped her collar and dragged her to his bed.

"Your entire revenge scheme is built on helping people. It's built on revenge for a woman who was lost to a set of circumstances and couldn't escape." Nicki stepped closer and cupped his cheek. "Don't you see? Our goals are the same."

"I don't just have a goal. I made a vow. I stood there and did nothing. I watched my mother die for nothing. Revenge is all I know." Peering into Nicki's eyes, he watched as tears fell. Pure tears, shed for him.

As they fell off her cheek and onto her shirt, he considered, for a fraction of a second, allowing her to help him. But tears couldn't sway his resolve and he sure as hell hadn't asked for her sympathy. "Time for you to leave. Don't come by here again, and if I see you around Korzakov, I'll stop you. You've revealed far too much about yourself, and I'll use that against you. Don't think I won't move you out of my way, because I will."

"Nice try." She shrugged. "Your threats don't faze me, because you're stupid and you're wrong."

That challenge was enough to bring forth everything Pavel had raised him to be. He grabbed both her wrists and slammed her against the refrigerator, pressing his erect cock against her hip. "Now that I think about it, I *can* see a benefit to our partnership." He rocked against her. "I'm sure you're a real good fuck. After all, you've had lots of practice." He ignored her swift intake of breath and kept pushing. "I bet there's nothing you won't do."

But she once again surprised him by laughing and then biting his lower lip hard before releasing it. "Are you trying to intimidate me by pressing against me with that small cock?"

Nicki bit down again until a burst of pain shot through his lip, and he tasted blood.

"You're right. I do know how to fuck a man." She licked her lips, smearing them with a drop of his blood. "But I need a good six inches, and honey, you ain't got much going for you, so thanks but no thanks. Back the hell off me, right now."

"No." But, oh, his primal side went with *yes*. He gripped her chin and kissed her, driving his tongue into that sweet, sugar-flavored mouth, because fuck her and her challenge. He meshed their lips together until the copper flavor from his bit lip burst on his tongue. Reveling in the mix of flavors, he tilted her head to the side, and pressed harder against her plump lips. This was heaven and hell. Light and darkness. And raw hunger like he'd never known before.

She kissed him back, gripping him tightly.

They were perfectly matched, each fighting for control. Breathing in each other's air. And the feeling fluttering in his heart was faint and unwanted so he nipped her bottom lip in retaliation.

Nicki shoved away, brushing a finger against her swollen lips. "Enough. You'd like that wouldn't you, getting a piece of me? Well you can chalk that up to never gonna happen, because you're a fool."

Hand against her chest, she sucked in a deep breath. "Someday you'll see the bigger picture, but until then, you keep on living in your small, empty, woe-is-me world and focus on your revenge and see where that gets you."

Damn her. She'd made him burn and ache and want. He needed her gone. Needed to quell this desire before he threw her over his shoulder and took her to his bedroom and buried himself so deep, that she'd understand the full meaning of "bigger picture." "How about you get out before I test your whole, 'never gonna happen' theory."

She arched a perfectly sculpted brow then headed for the door. Halfway there, she stopped and glanced over her shoulder. "Have you ever considered who you are without the revenge? And what happens if someone gets to Korzakov before you? I'll leave my offer open. I could use your financial backing on this."

After adjusting his throbbing cock, he followed her path into the living room and leaned against the back of his black leather couch. "And here I thought you were done working for money?"

"Oh, good one." She fake-laughed and slapped her knee. "Such a burn. I'm so hurt. Sticks and stones, you broke my bones or however that saying goes. Your attempt at an insult didn't work. Just like your attempt at a kiss...it sucked. That thing you did with your tongue was worse than the time my mother's second husband held me down and tried to shove his down my throat."

So they were doing this again. The last time they worked together, they played this little who-had-the-most-horrific-childhood game. Her statements might not be real, but his were. "I'm sure it was better than the time Pavel held *me* down and tattooed a star on my shoulder so if I ever went to prison, I'd have the symbol of authority as a warning."

"Whatever. The kiss was awful, and you smell like a girl."

"What?" He dipped his chin and sniffed his armpit.

"Lavender? I mean, what are you a florist? And I *told* you to stop saying, 'what!'"

"It's lavender *and* cedar. If you're going to insult someone, at least get it right."

"Take your lavender and your cedar and shove them both up your ass." Lifting her middle finger, she sailed out the door.

And for five minutes, he stood and stared at the closed door, until he finally figured out why he couldn't move.

She'd lied.

She *had* kissed him back, clawing against his bare back and holding on for dear life.

But that realization couldn't matter.

Yet for a moment, he closed his eyes and remembered her taste and the softness of her lips. And hadn't he heard a soft whimper? All of the above was why he'd walked away from her before and hadn't looked back.

And now the door was shut between them again, and he'd never ever open it.

CHAPTER THREE

After taking a sip from his dark roast coffee, Korzakov narrowed his eyes at the man in the seat across from his desk. This office in the back of one of his many restaurants was the only place he'd foul with this pervert's presence. The wondrous smell of garlic and tomato sauce filtering in from the other side of the door did nothing to cover the fact that this man sullied the air just by breathing.

The tall redhead with the scar around his neck had obviously taken a beaten by someone. The man claimed Erik Pavel was the perpetrator.

No matter.

Korzakov would do the same, likely far worse, once done using McCord as a way to get under Erik's skin. Plus, he liked using McCord to torment Sheridan Bennett. Let that Hollywood bitch worry he'd let loose the reigns on this dog, and her sister, Jenny would die just like his sister, Maria had. A fitting end, and one he'd see through when he finished his business with Erik Pavel.

With a slight wince, McCord shifted in his seat. "So, you won't speak to Erik about this?" He waved a hand at his bruised face. "All I said was that I wanted to see Jenny. And what does Erik do? He ties me to a chair and beats me. Then Sheridan saunters her pregnant ass into the warehouse, and he lets her hit me, too. I won't work with Erik anymore. I'm finished. He doesn't understand my need to see Jenny. No one does."

Korzakov sniffed. "This is true. Your desires are revolting."

"Jenny" was McCord's biological daughter, and after fifteen years in jail for almost killing Sheridan Bennett—now an award-winning actress—McCord spared no love for his daughter's older half-sister. Every time McCord caught a glimpse of Sheridan's pictures in the tabloids, he'd rant for hours and hours. He'd revealed a lot of interesting information on Sheridan Bennett and their shared past. Her wanting a bit of her own back against McCord made absolutely sense. He *had* molested the movie star as a child, after all. Who knew what the sick bastard had planned for his teen-aged daughter, Jenny after all these years.

"I'll kill that blonde bitch after I finish with Erik. She thinks she can take a shot at me and get away with it. Her lies are what put me in prison to begin with."

"Yes, I've heard your story ad nauseam. And no, you're not touching a single strand on the golden girl's head. Do I need to remind you why?"

McCord sputtered.

"Shut up." Korzakov held up a hand. "Sheridan Bennett's father killed my sister therefore Sheridan will die by my hand, and my hand alone. You serve only one purpose, and that is..." Korzakov circled his hand in the air, arching a brow at the man before him.

"To discover Erik's plans."

"Yes. *That* is your only reason for breathing. Do *not* forget it. Plus, your inept revenge plans against Sheridan Bennett will only bring her detective fiancé, Clayton Kincaid to my door. So, you'll let me handle things as we agreed, yes?"

McCord paused for a moment, running a finger along his jagged scar.

"Answer me. My patience is thinning."

"Yes, fine."

Korzakov tapped his phone against his open palm. "I need Erik more than I need you. The fact that he's blood thirsty and finds it necessary to keep you in check doesn't trouble me in the least."

"He's stopped working for you."

"He thinks he has." Korzakov shrugged and then sipped from his coffee cup. "Everyone thinks they can betray me and take what's mine, but I'm sixty-seven and I've seen it all. I know all about his alliances. I know he's working with the FBI. But no matter, because so am I. Who doesn't? How do you think I stay out of jail?"

"I don't know about all that. I just came in here to ask for justice. Erik beat me, and then that bitch came in..." McCord grumbled more indecipherable words under his breath and rubbed his beefy paws together.

Korzakov sent a text to Yegor asking him to return to the office. After reviewing a few more texts, he faced McCord again. "I'm sorry, I wasn't listening. You may leave now."

McCord bent forward, his shoe shuffling back and forth across the tile floor. "I only want to see my daughter. Sheridan has no business interfering. She's not mine, but Jenny is, and I have a right to see my own blood. You promised to help me get her and so far, you haven't followed through."

Korzakov lifted a hand. "Be careful how you speak to me, or your current condition will seem like nothing."

A knock sounded on the door, and then Yegor entered. "Sir?"

"Yegor, I thought you might like to see Erik's handiwork."

Yegor glanced at McCord and laughed. "That is all. I could do so much more."

McCord shrank in his seat.

Coward.

This man preyed on little girls but when faced with someone his own size, he trembled in fear. "Yegor, I don't know that I believe you. I want you to show me."

"What?" McCord's eyes went wide. "I'll leave. I don't need Yegor to show you anything." He shot to his feet and dashed to the door.

Yegor gripped the back of his shirt and spun him around. Then his thick fist connected with McCord's face.

The sound of flesh hitting flesh was music to Korzakov's ears. "Again, Yegor. I'm not convinced."

McCord yelped and lifted both hands to cover his face.

Yegor punched the side of McCord's head again.

Sporting a full grin, Korzakov rounded the desk. "Continue."

Yegor struck McCord, over and over until the man dropped to his knees. Blood flew from the man's mouth and trickled down his nose. His screams perfectly complimented Yegor's grunts.

Damn. Korzakov's own ears rang just imagining the pain. "All right! Enough, Yegor. I'm convinced."

Yegor released his grip on McCord's bloody face before tugging on his cock through his dress pants, obviously turned on by the violence.

Korzakov straightened his suit jacket and smiled at Yegor. "Such a bloodthirsty one. I love it." He patted Yegor's shoulder. "Lunch should be ready shortly, and after that you deserve a treat. We'll go to the club, and you may choose any girl you'd like."

"Yes, sir." Yegor nodded. "Thank you, sir."

Yegor was certainly loyal. During a trip home to Russia, Korzakov had plucked him and his brother, Georgy from the streets and made them his own. Not as sons, necessarily, they weren't intelligent enough to take over his empire, but they were certainty capable of protecting it.

"Nicely done." Korzakov glanced down at the moaning man, who had both hands covering his ears. "McCord, all I need from you is to keep an eye on Erik. That's all I've ever asked. I didn't ask you to cry over a couple of bruises. I asked you to watch him, and if you can't do that, you're of no use to me." Korzakov reared back and kicked McCord in the ribs.

The man shrieked then tumbled to his side.

"You will tell me where Erik goes, who he meets. That is all I need. As far as your daughter, I'd need more personnel to follow and capture her than I can spare right now."

McCord started to laugh. A manic laugh of a man pushed over the edge. He spit blood on the floor and rose to his knees. "Erik's beating. Yegor's beating. They are nothing compared to what I endured in prison. Do you know what they did to me? I endured horrors you can't imagine."

Korzakov bent closer to McCord. "You see, McCord. That's where you're wrong. I *can* imagine." He grabbed his half-full coffee cup off the desk and tipped the still steaming brew onto McCord's leg.

"Ahhh! Damn it!" McCord scrambled to his feet, clutching his side and wiping at the wet spot on his khaki pants.

Korzakov whipped the cup at McCord, striking his shoulder. "Understand this, I don't care what you've suffered. If you touch your daughter or any other child inappropriately, I'll know, and I'll end you. Do not come into my presence again. You will contact Yegor from now on. You disgust me."

"B-but what about my daughter? I-I need her, and you promised."

Korzakov shook his head before facing Yegor. "Yegor, give this man your contact information then see him out." After waiting for Yegor's nod, he left the room, strolling into the kitchen. He peered over the lead chef's shoulder, inhaling deeply. "Smells delicious. Is it almost done?"

The man kept his focus forward. "Yes, sir. This is the first time I've ever made tamales. Was a nice change."

"Good man." Korzakov clapped him on the shoulder.

This chef was known for his exquisite Italian dishes, not Mexican cuisine. But Korzakov had asked for a meal in honor of his guest today. A man who would help destroy his enemies, because based on the underground rumblings, they were making their move soon.

Let them come. He was older, wiser, and certainly more ruthless. No one would knock him from his throne. And if he had to dine with a greasy border rat in order to maintain his kingdom, so be it.

CHAPTER FOUR

"Your brother kissed me." Nicki sank against the sandwich shop's booth and met Rachel Harris's gaze across the table.

Her friend—okay, sort of friend—froze with a spoon loaded with broccoli cheese soup at her lips before she blinked and her pert nose wrinkled. With her petite frame, soft brown hair, and almond-shaped brown eyes, Rachel tricked a person into believing she was a harmless little pixie, when actually she owned a detective agency and was a total badass.

And now that Nicki considered the are-they-really-friends question, she felt her stomach twist a little. Was this a friendship? Why had she mentioned the kiss to Erik's sister of all people?

"Umm...I thought you and Erik were dating or whatever...so, I'm sorry, but I'm confused." Rachel dropped her spoon back in the bowl.

"No, we aren't together." Nicki fiddled with the straw in her cup. "Haven't been together. I'll be straight with you. We only worked together to uncover Ariel's plans for that football player, and then I sort of helped Erik with some information I had on...someone."

"Someone? Like who?"

"Use your interrogation skills on someone else, Rachel."

"Do I need to use them?"

"What are you now? A lawyer like your uncle?"

"Do I need to be?"

Nicki rolled her eyes and dug into her bags of Cheetos. This conversation was likely why she had few friends. People drove her crazy. But Rachel was one of the most "authentic" people she'd ever met, and very loyal, because hadn't the woman searched for her brother her whole life? Nicki could do with a few genuine friends, so Rachel Harris was worth the aggravation.

"Back to the issue at hand. So my brother kissed you, and...?" Rachel rolled her hand in the air. "Why are you bringing that up? Does he have two tongues or something? No, I know, it's forked, isn't it?" She chuckled before mumbling, "Wouldn't surprise me."

Nicki laughed then shook her head. "No forks, actually the kiss was more of a dominance thing. Like, 'don't test me or I'll smash your face with my face'. Which is ridiculous. Basically he *wanted* to kiss me. Probably has for a long time, and he waited until he could do so as a scare tactic...or whatever, because then it's okay in his mind. Men are so stupid." And the kiss was stupid. And sucked. And she thought about it every day.

"And you?" Rachel asked the question in a soft tone, her head slightly tilted.

"And me, what?" Inviting Rachel to lunch after her friend's brow waxing appointment was maybe not the best idea when Nicki had all these stupid fluttering emotions rolling through her system.

"Did you want Erik to kiss you?"

"What?" Nicki snorted and glanced at the people in line at the counter. She refused to meet Rachel's eyes because...Well, crap. She *had* invited this interrogation, so why not spill? "I don't even know why I brought up the stupid kiss. The whole thing is pointless." She sighed. "I mean, I guess you could say he's attractive, all dark brown hair, and broody brown eyes, and that trim body, and his ass, I mean... he must work out all the time to...um...what was I saying?"

Rachel broke into a wide grin.

"Shut up." Nicki felt her cheeks heat. "Anyway, your brother may be gorgeous, but he's a total asshole. He refuses any help with his stupid scheme, and he'll likely get himself killed. Plus, living in that world, he's damaging his soul so deeply, he'll never recover. And why do I care? Why? But he and I...We're just...for some reason I don't understand, I can't give up on him." After the brutal events that led to her leaving the escort service, and then Ariel's betrayal, Nicki hadn't had much belief in anything anymore, until a few women in prison had formed a support group of sorts. Within that circle, she'd learned that no matter what, her life had meaning, and she could serve a greater purpose. With that thought in mind now, she mentally checked her upcoming calendar, because she hadn't visited her prison friends in a few weeks, and she'd promised to return as often as possible.

Those women had played a pivotal part in making her believe in herself again, and she wouldn't forget that. "When I was in prison, I hated everyone, hated myself. Ariel had destroyed my heart. But the women in there, they took me under their wing and made me want to fight again." Nicki wiped at the tear on her cheek. "I don't have much, but I can listen. I can volunteer. I can hold a hand. I can offer a hug. I can help women, and Erik has a means to help too. He has to see that."

Rachel reached across the table and took her hand. "Erik is very... hard, and you need to know he is also very brutal. Which is...I just wish his life could've been different." Rachel slumped in her seat before fiddling with her spoon. "Did you talk to Andrea Martin at Turning Pages?"

"Not yet, but I will."

"Good. She recently started a program with a local tattoo parlor. They cover up the tattoos or basically *brands* that pimps put on their women. Andrea is good people. Perhaps helping her raise funds might...I don't know, help you."

"Turning Pages helps survivors of trafficking and prostitution, right? Helps them with training for jobs and such?"

"Yes, Andrea is also working on raising enough funds to provide temporary housing units."

"Ever think she'd do more?"

Rachel crumbled a saltine cracker over her soup bowl. "In what way?"

"Never mind." Nicki wrapped up her sandwich.

"Hey. Don't go." Rachel grabbed her arm. "Explain. What do you mean by *more?*"

Nicki huffed out a breath and leaned forward. "I mean, shouldn't we go after the source? Shouldn't we go after the organizations causing all the problems? Is Andrea Martin willing to take on people like Otari Korzakov? That's where we need to focus."

"We?" Rachel's brow furrowed. "As in you've already started focusing there?"

"Yes, I asked your brother for help. You'd think after what happened with his mother he'd be more amenable to having a little assistance, but no, he has to do it all alone like a super asshole."

"He is an ass."

Nicki released a long sigh. "He's stuck, ya know? He could do so much more with his life. Use his anger and hate and pain for something good."

"He doesn't know any other way."

"Really, you're defending him?"

"In a way, yes. I lost him, and so everything he is today is my fault."

"Rachel, don't—"

"No." Rachel dropped her gaze and ran an index finger along the table's edge. "He was my responsibility, and I-I...I lost him. He was just this little guy, only three years old, and I walked away to use that park bathroom, and when I came back out...he was gone. Victor Pavel stole my brother from me and raised him to be ruthless, heartless, and deadly. That's all Erik knows. And that's on me. I wish more than anything that wasn't true but it is. I wish he would let go of the past. That he and I could be a family. But he's made very clear he doesn't want that...and it hurts. A lot." She rubbed a hand across her breast-bone. "I finally found him and he's still so far out of reach. Whatever you're hoping to get from him...if you have feelings for him, I'd caution you against them, because, and I'm sorry to say this, but he isn't capable of loving you as he should. I'm afraid he's too far gone."

"Uh, what?" Heart pounding, Nicki straightened in her seat. "I never said I wanted him to love me."

"Then what has this whole conversation been about?"

"Not that." Nicki scoffed over the ridiculousness of Rachel's comment, yet her heart continued to flip.

"Are you sure?"

"I know more about Erik's world than you do, Rachel. I lived in it for years."

"Okay." Elbows on the table, Rachel held up both hands, palms outward. "I'm not trying to upset you. I agree he could do so much more with his life, but I don't think it's possible. I'd hate for you to get your hopes up."

Hope. That one word could mean so much and yet cut so deep. And regardless of what Rachel said, Nicki maintained a small slither for Erik. When he'd kissed her, she'd felt a flare of passion. He wouldn't try so hard to push her away if he wasn't afraid of her in some way. "I hear what you're saying, Rachel. But honestly, your brother hides behind his revenge plot so he doesn't have to live, but he saved you, and he helped me with Ariel. He has a heart buried in there somewhere."

"Don't let those glimmers blind you to who he really is, Nicki."

"I'm not." But they both knew she kind of was...

CHAPTER FIVE

A few mornings after his run-in with Nicki, Erik stopped at the gas station down the street from his apartment. Walking across the lot to his car, he sipped from his gas station coffee. He and McCord had a job today—threatening a lawyer, who needed a reminder that Korzakov expected loyalty. Seemed to Erik a gun to the head would serve much better than these petty slaps.

Erik set the steaming to-go cup on top of his gold '77 Monte Carlo and unlocked the door. Temps were supposed to hit the upper eighties today, which matched his own level of fury at having to spend the day with a disgusting pedophile.

The already humid air was filled with the stench of gas and rotting garbage. He hated coming to this side of town. Reaching for his coffee, he stilled as the hairs on the back of his neck rose.

"Pavel." A familiar voice spoke, the underlying anger evident in the tone. "So nice to see you out and about, and all alone."

He'd been waiting for this visit, expecting it even, because he would do the exact same thing if he were in the man's position.

Without turning around, Erik grabbed his coffee from the car's hood, bending to put it on the car's floor mat. "Are we having this discussion in a gas station parking lot? Seems a little out in the open."

"As if you give a shit where or when?"

Erik turned and stared into the icy blue eyes of a very pissed Clayton Kincaid.

"Sheridan is fucking pregnant." Clayton stormed forward, jaw clenched, fists balled up tight, and menace in his eyes. "Pregnant! Does that mean anything to you? Does that register at all in your deluded mind?"

Erik shoved a hand in his dress pants pocket, because when cornered, wild animals attacked. He didn't want to hurt Clayton— but he would. "How did you find me?"

Clayton jabbed a finger in Erik's face. "Stay away from Sheridan, and Jenny for that matter."

"I intend—"

"I don't want to hear it." Clayton lifted a hand. "Any further issues with McCord, you come to me." He turned that jabbing finger to his own chest. "I'll handle him."

Erik should leave it at that. What did he care? Hadn't Pavel beat into his head that he owed no one any explanations for his actions. His mantra: *A real man never explained.* Erik knew this, yet he found himself rooted in place. Taking a moment to think through how he wanted this exchange to play out, Erik retrieved his coffee then leaned against the driver's side door. After all, *he* hadn't told Ms. Bennett to put surveillance on McCord. *He* hadn't told Ms. I've-got-money-to-spare-on-spy gadgets to follow him to that abandoned warehouse. And he hadn't suggested she strike McCord that day. "I didn't ask Sheridan to be there, but I can't deny she deserved to have that moment."

Clayton hauled back and punched him in the jaw.

Coffee went flying, luckily none landed on his suit.

"Goddamnit! Don't you tell me what Sheridan deserves. You let her be in the same room as that monster! She's pregnant, you stupid son of a bitch. What if something had happened to her or the baby? What the fuck is wrong with you?"

Erik rubbed his aching jaw and took a moment to find some inner calm, because when he got hit, he hit back. Normally he wouldn't refrain, but he respected this man. Clayton deserved to have a say, but one hit was all Erik would take. Just one. "Clayton, I can't help but think your anger stems from the fact that *you* didn't get a moment with McCord, but I didn't owe you that. Sheridan is the wild card here, not me."

"You don't know anything about her."

"Oh, but I do." Erik picked up the empty to-go cup and tossed it in the trash. He had enough adrenaline to make it through the day now. Fuck caffeine. Wiping his hands on his pants, he faced Clayton again. "Sheridan is a pull-the-trigger-first kind of woman, and you... you think of all the repercussions before you let that bullet fly. Sheridan is raw, hard, and battle scarred. You...well, we both know you've got good ole lawman running through your veins."

Clayton ran a hand over his face, scrubbing his eyes before he met Erik's gaze again. "Do me a favor and don't tell *me* who Sheridan is and who she isn't. That just pisses me off even more. She isn't you."

"She's a lot more me than she is you."

"You have no idea when to shut up, do you?" Clayton threw up both hands and shook his head.

Erik grinned. "It's part of my charm."

Clayton rubbed two fingers against his forehead. "The point is, I know what you've done. Whether you think I do or not, I know you're the reason Korzakov hasn't come after Sheridan in retaliation for her father's actions." He braced both hands on his hips. "Listen, I know what it's like to lose someone you love. Only..." He sighed. "I need you to hear me when I say this, regardless of what we've both been through, if anything were to happen to Sheridan and my unborn child, I would destroy whoever was responsible. You may think I wouldn't pull the trigger, but don't test me." He ran a hand through his thick dark brown hair. "I appreciate your help distracting Korzakov, I really do, but stay away from Sheridan."

"I suggest you level your argument to her, not me." Erik knew Clayton had lost a younger brother. He'd discovered as much during his investigations. After all, he couldn't let just anyone be his sister's partner. "I advised Sheridan to leave town...and yet..." Erik waved a hand at Clayton. "McCord has very serious designs on Jenny, and with Korzakov's help, he'll achieve his goal. So, instead of finding me, you need to find your way out of town."

Clayton rapped his knuckles against the car's roof. "You really couldn't call me? Couldn't give me a shot at McCord?"

"I've already explained my reasoning." Erik tugged his keys from the front pocket of his pants. "If we're retreading points I've already covered, I'd prefer to leave."

"Once again, she's pregnant."

"Momma bears are fierce."

"Fuck you, Pavel."

"So eloquent." Erik flipped the keys around on its keychain. "Be original, and listen to what I'm saying. I'll repeat it again, because apparently, you aren't hearing me. Get out of town."

Clayton leaned against his door and crossed both arms over his chest. "When my brother died, I went after the men who watched him die outside that restaurant. I know about payback." He shook his head and stared out across the lot. "I also know that hunting down those guys and beating them didn't bring back my brother." He heaved a long sigh. "Don't fight against Korzakov on your own. Let me help. Let Rachel help. Let's do this the right way. The legal way."

Erik huffed out a laugh. "Do you know how many people Korzakov owns? And if he doesn't, he will. I don't want or need your help. Go home to your girls, pack, leave, and I'll let you know when this is over."

Clayton kicked the Monte Carlo's tire and stood back, hand on his hips. "Nice car. Gold, really?"

"It's pure gangster."

Clayton chuckled then scratched the back of his neck. "Once McCord got out of jail, Sheridan and I put safety measures in place."

"The most secure wall can be breached."

"You work with McCord?"

Erik sniffed. "I do."

Clayton nodded. "Then tell him this, and maybe you should listen, too. Sheridan is my life and anything that affects her, affects me."

"Fine." Erik opened his car door and sank into his seat, sideways. "You're a good man, Kincaid. Congratulations on the child and all that."

"You could have the same."

"What? A child?"

"No, a family."

"My family died."

"Don't think so. You have a sister and two parents still alive."

"Would you mind?" Erik motioned for Clayton to move away from his car. "I'm finished with this conversation."

Clayton bent and studied the tire. "This looks a little flat." He patted the rim. "Might want to get some air before you're off."

Erik rolled his eyes. "Are you through investigating my car *and* me?"

"No." Clayton grinned. "Whether you like it or not, Rachel and I are helping you."

Erik shoved his keys in the ignition and revved up the engine. "Stay out of my business, because in case you've forgotten, I can get to your woman. Sheridan and I, we shared a moment. If I call, she'll come."

"Nice try, Pavel, but I see you." Clayton pointed two fingers at his eyes and then darted them back in Erik's direction.

Erik shoved the car in reverse and left behind not only the lot but also Clayton's words about family, because those dreams had ended long ago.

THAT EVENING, Erik tossed his cards onto the table. With four Queens and an Ace, he'd won the pot. A pounding bass from the nightclub below this makeshift office shook the walls—and his innards, or maybe that sensation came from nerves. His current situation was filled with every kind of danger and every move carefully calculated.

Cardboard boxes of alcohol filled the room, and the scent of Frankie's Cuban cigar filtered through the air. A grouping of about ten of Frankie's men were sprawled across a beat-up, maroon U-shaped sectional with a few scantily-dressed women on their laps. They all shared a couple bottles of high-end scotch. The sweet scent of marijuana drifted over to their rickety table from time to time, and Erik wondered how much of their product they actually sampled. At least they weren't delving into something heavier, like cocaine. Erik didn't believe Castillo ran his business like that. His only vice seemed to be expensive cigars.

Frankie Castillo liked to play poker while they talked business. Said he could read anybody over a game of cards. Erik doubted that. While unwise to win against such a deadly man, Erik did it anyway. Never back down was another mantra Pavel had literally pounded into his head.

Castillo, a thirty-year old immigrant from Mexico, had started his rise to power in southern California. Then he moved to Ohio in order to be at, "the Crossroads of America." Erik had explained that Indiana bore that title, and Castillo had shrugged him off.

Short in stature, Castillo had dark hair and eyes, and tattoos covering his body. The man had forged an agreement of sorts with Korzakov. They each had their territories, their ongoing scams, and they generally tried to steer clear of one another—all while secretly concocting plans to bring the other down.

"And you win again." Frankie shook his head. "Still can't read you. I can read everybody, but not you. You know what that means, right?"

Erik shrugged. "Nothing except I'm good at cards." He straightened the deck before pushing a bowl of peanuts to the side.

"Or you're a sociopath."

"Never been one for labels."

"What label would you give Nicki Nobles?"

Erik almost stiffened before catching himself. *Show no tells.* He picked up an Ace and tapped it against the table. "Don't go there."

"I haven't, but Pavel seems...interested." Frankie eased back in his seat. "I thought she was yours. Women...meh, can't trust them."

"Exactly." Erik wouldn't answer one way or another about Nicki. Better she remained a non-topic. Korzakov hounding her was bad enough, but Castillo catching her scent was much, much worse. Erik would have time to counter any moves Korzakov made against Nicki, but the same couldn't be said for Castillo. Frankie generally eradicated complications—immediately and lethally.

"One more game." Castillo plucked the Ace from Erik's hand— literally and figuratively.

The gangster had shown his own winning hand by mentioning Nicki. So, Erik would play another round, because *this* was the game that mattered. The first was just a warm up and was apparently played in order to issue some kind of warning. One Erik would heed.

Castillo was sure his office was bugged so exchanging money over cards was an innocuous way for Erik to pay him. Every word they spoke from here on out would hold a double meaning.

Castillo shuffled the deck before signaling the two men who'd been hovering at his back. "Raul and Chaz, join us."

Erik nodded his greeting as the tattooed men took their seats. Each tattoo held a special significance or meaning. When incarcerated, these marks alerted others to their affiliations on the outside, which meant protection on the inside.

Erik's only tattoo was the blue star on his shoulder. Put there by

Pavel as a way to signify his position in the Russian mafia should he ever be unlucky enough to serve prison time. Ironic that he'd killed Pavel, along with others, and never had to use this mark his father deemed necessary. Others had taken the blame, something if he thought on too much, he might actually be grateful to Korzakov for.

"You keep winning, but you might lose this hand." Castillo glanced at Erik as he dealt cards to each player.

Knowing Castillo actually meant losing against Korzakov, Erik was careful in his reply. "Can't win if you don't play."

"This is true." Castillo turned his gaze to his cards. "Let's focus on this game."

Erik skimmed his cards, ready to get to the business at hand.

"Last time I looked through this deck, I found a Joker."

Erik knew Castillo referred to a couple low-level addicts who had somehow gotten their hands on a "skimmer" and were using it in Castillo's territory. A person did not do business in Castillo's territory without permission—and most weren't brave enough to ask.

Erik had already tracked the addicts down, but as strung out as they were, they likely wouldn't remember his warnings. So, he'd taken their device and their cache of stolen debit cards and left them. Not much else he could do. They were already skin and bones and rotted teeth. As he'd left the abandoned building, he wondered how they'd been smart enough to set up the skimmer at a gas station. Maybe they'd just happened upon it. Who knew with desperate junkies?

Erik shuffled his cards, putting them in numeric order. "I sometimes find two Joker's when looking through a deck, but they get tossed aside, and I don't see them again."

Castillo nodded before removing another cigar from his shirt pocket and stuffing the hefty end into his mouth.

Raul glanced at Castillo then stood, striding into the other room as he dialed a number on his phone. Maybe to verify Erik's information on the junkies, maybe not.

Castillo had all sorts of scams running at all times. The usual, like gambling, loansharking, extortion, drug running and dealing. He'd added a few white-collar crimes to his dossier, like credit card fraud, so having two nobodies in his territory raised a red flag. Plus, Castillo liked sending messages to those attempting to set up shop in his area. Bloody messages. Loss-of-limb-messages. But Erik didn't need that kind of heat coming down on Castillo right now. So, after hearing about these two fools from a source, he'd handled it as a favor. That's how things worked in his world. A favor for a favor.

Raul returned and the card game went smoothly after that with Erik purposefully losing twenty-five grand. The final payment on their deal. Castillo's contacts in Mexico would now make sure Korzakov's cocaine and heroin shipments didn't cross the border. A dicey business that Castillo planned to blame on local gangs—which were controlled by his cousin.

Erik eased back in his chair. "Nice game. We'll see you in a week."

"No. I have other plans."

Erik stilled. Any changes in arrangements at this point were unexpected and unwelcome. Erik eyed the other two men at the table and considered how quickly he could remove his gun from his shoulder holster.

"My daughter turns twenty-one next week. We're hosting a fiesta in Las Vegas. I want you there, and I want you to bring Nicki along."

Erik arched a brow. "Why would I do that?"

"Because I asked you, cabrón."

"She's nothing. Otari's ex-whore." He hated using the word, but better he use it than for Castillo to believe she meant anything.

"If that is the case then bringing her shouldn't be a problem. Women like the glitter of Vegas."

"I find no reason to bring her." Jaw clenched, Erik picked up a peanut and crushed it between his fingers, envisioning Castillo's head in its place. "She and I finished our business months ago."

Castillo stood from the table. "She'll come because I've asked it of you."

Erik kept Castillo's gaze for a moment before nodding. "We'll see."

"That we will, Pavel. That we will."

CHAPTER SIX

Holding both hands at her sides so she didn't blacken Erik's eyes, Nicki tried finding her calm place. Hitting people was apparently frowned upon. But breaking behaviors learned at childhood wasn't easy—or in this case, welcome.

Nicki glared across the massage table, taking a few deep breaths and cursing her decision to become a better person. How dare Erik show up in the middle of her workday and ask for help. A small part of her wanted to scream, 'I told you so', but she refrained. After tossing out her now tasteless bubble gum, she rounded on Erik, poking a finger in his direction. "Days ago, you kicked me out of your place, and that was before you threatened me with your dick, and now you want me to go to Vegas? Are you mental?"

"I don't understand what the big deal is. It's a free trip."

He leaned against her countertop, looking all GQ in his black suit and gold tie, which highlighted his stupid brown eyes, which she still wanted to punch then maybe kiss and make better.

"Free for whom?" Nicki straightened the maroon blanket on her table. "I'm sure *some* cost is involved. Some way. Somehow. Because you made clear you weren't interested in me...I-I mean, m-my plan." *Crap!* Why had she let that slip? "So what's the angle, Pavel?"

"I never said I wasn't..." He sighed and rubbed his forehead. "Will you just listen, please? I feel bad about how I left things with you, and I need to go to Vegas, so I thought you could come with me. That's all."

"Sure. Uh-huh...*You* are a liar." She pointed at the open door. "Please leave because some of us have legitimate jobs to do, and you're stinking up my space with your girly lavender *and cedar* perfume."

Erik sighed before rounding the table and standing before her. "I've thought about what you said, and I think you're right, we should work together. I was wrong before."

"Wow." Nicki stepped back and started clapping. "Oscar worthy performance, really. But my workplace isn't a stage, Pavel, and you're a shit actor, so get your lying ass out of my face."

"I'm not lying." He lifted his chin and met her gaze.

"Yeah, you are." Nicki pressed a finger right between his eyes and shoved. "No way are you suddenly interested without some ulterior motive. You'd *never* admit to being wrong. This trip is about you and your stupid revenge scheme. I asked for your help and you said no, so here's *my* no back. We got a whole lot of no's between us, so how's about we keep it that way?" She planted a hand on her hip and lifted a finger in the air, waving it back and forth. "Nope. Nada. Nyet. Buh-bye."

"All right, okay." He captured her finger and pressed her hand back to her side. "Listen, you're involved in this now."

"In *this*?" Her heart thumped a little, because whatever reason had him here, practically begging at her door, had to be bad. Very bad. "What do you mean by *this*? You wanted no *involvement*, so don't be throwing that word around like we have anything between us."

Erik raked his fingers through his thick hair. "Certain...people... know about you."

"People? What people?"

"When I said I was wrong, I meant it." Erik braced a hip against her massage table. "We never should have partnered for that Ariel thing, because now people think you mean something to me."

"I'm sorry, but I'm not understanding you." Maybe she should use one of her waxing Q-tips to clean her ears, because, after her lunch with Rachel, she'd taken a hard look at her future and decided Erik Pavel wouldn't be in it. But now, her stupid heart fluttered a little. Plus Erik Pavel in a suit...goodness gracious, she needed a hand fan. A well-dressed man apparently did it for her, which seemed odd considering that most of her ex-clients were businessmen—or women. But she'd never been clear-headed where Erik was concerned. "Would you mind speaking like a normal person versus whatever bad guy lingo you're using right now?"

Erik lifted his chin and stared at the ceiling while shaking his head. "Why? Why me?"

Nicki narrowed her eyes. "Don't act like *I'm* the pain in the ass in this scenario."

He nodded, sobering quickly. "Because of our previous arrangement, you're a target now. My enemies see you as my weakness even if we both know that's ludicrous."

"That's an understatement." However, using her to hurt him did make sense in a way. They *had* been together a lot. But what did any of this have to do with a trip to Vegas? "Korzakov already—"

"This isn't about him. The threat is coming from someone else."

"Someone else?"

"Yeah."

"Care to elaborate?"

"Not really."

"So someone is gunning for me, but you don't care to tell me who. Well...then...you can leave because *I* have work to do." She lifted her appointment book off the counter then released it so it landed with a plop. Of course, her hand shook a little, because...he'd put her in the cross hairs of "someone." And likely they would do terrible, painful things to her person before tossing her into some barn with starving pigs or burying her in a ditch where skunks would chew on her rotting flesh. "Running off to Vegas to play your games isn't in the cards...Ha! See what I just did there?"

Shaking his head, he sighed then ran a hand down his tie. "It's safer if you went with me."

"Safer?"

"These guys don't mess around, Nicki. I'm close, so close. One wrong move will ruin everything."

When he'd first arrived, she'd just wanted him to leave, but now she was a little scared and a whole lot pissed, because what the hell had he dragged her into? Sure, she'd known she would court danger by going after traffickers, but that was her choice. Erik guiding her life in any way rubbed her wrong. "Plan B, Pavel. Ever heard of that? Anytime you do something, you always need a Plan B. Hell, have a Plan C. It's what all the super villains are doing these days. Join the club."

"That's right, I *am* a villain." He eased closer, circling her wrist with his hand.

Sparks flared, but, nope, not happening. Nicki pressed a hand against his muscled chest. "Back off."

Ignoring her warning, he leaned closer and spoke against her ear. "Listen very carefully. I know a lot of people in this town. People who know people at the Ohio State Board of Cosmetology or Sanitation or whatever governs your little business. They might find it necessary to pay you a visit."

She shoved him away—and the shiver he'd elicited. "And there it is. You've just hit rock bottom. Do you realize what you've done?"

"What's that?" He eased back, eyes narrowed.

"You've destroyed any belief I had that you contained a shred of decency. Gone. Poof."

"I never asked you to believe in me. I've always made clear who I am."

"Yeah, that's crystal clear." She shook her head, more sorry than she should ever be over a hopeless case like him. "Do your worst, Pavel. Go ahead. Threaten me. Threaten my place of business. Because the thing is, I've been held at gunpoint and cut with a knife. I've been beat down, left bloody and bruised, and guess what? I get up again. I fight. I asked you to fight with me, and you said no. So as far as I see it, that was the end for you and me."

"Nicki, I know what you think of me, and you're right about everything, but you *will* come to Vegas even if I have to drag you there by your hair."

She studied him a moment, noticing for the first time the light grayish-purple shade under his eyes and his unshaven chin. Interesting. Perhaps he was showing a little wear and tear. Revenge plots apparently took a lot out of a man. "Why should you care if I'm in danger? What's it to you?"

"It's...it's not about that. I don't..." Releasing a low growl, he turned for the door then glanced over his shoulder. "Friday at five. Be packed and ready."

"I will shoot you in the ass if you come anywhere near me on Friday."

A knock sounded against her open door.

Her next appointment stepped through her doorway, staring at Erik with wide eyes and a dropped jaw.

"Good afternoon." He grinned at the practically drooling woman before turning back to Nicki and winking. "See you Friday."

The older blonde fanned her faced with her phone. "Well, now, wasn't he something?"

"Oh." Nicki dug her nails into her palm. "He's something all right."

CHAPTER SEVEN

"Thanks, Sarah." Erik smiled as the waitress filled his coffee cup. Sarah was a staple at this hole-in-the-wall diner, just like he was. Her gait was a bit slower now, and her hair a bit grayer. The skin around her lips created a wrinkled pout due to years of smoking. Maybe inhaling grease-filled air was the secret to a long life, because she should've keeled over long before now. Every time he came in, she gave him hell, but that was just her way. It was also her way to slip him a piece of pie on occasion, to fatten him up, she'd say.

His mother had brought him here as a kid. Late nights spent eating syrup-laden pancakes and enjoying the quiet time away from their nightmare life. Victor Pavel hadn't been kind to either of them. He'd molded and shaped. He'd used his fists to dominate and to teach very real lessons. Painful lessons—ones that not only scarred the body but also the soul.

Abducted from one family then thrown into another, Erik had found some solace with his teenage mother, Katya who knew no more about love and kindness than he did. But they'd protected one another as best they could.

Until the bullet ripped through her chest.

Until the blood stained her pink shirt.

And that swath of hair covered her face and he couldn't move.

Korzakov would pay for pulling the trigger.

The bells hanging on the diner's door jangled.

From Erik's position in the farthest booth, he watched as US Marshal Leonard Moore sauntered toward him. The lawman was around six-three, slim, with greying hair in a buzz cut.

Leonard tipped his black cowboy hat toward Sarah before sliding across from him.

"Leonard."

"Pavel."

Erik held back a sigh. They frequently met at this diner. Leonard served as his contact for the FBI and other agencies. Erik has also been under the Marshal's protective custody a few times over the years. After Pavel's death. And for a short time after Erik had assisted Rachel. But he'd left again, since hiding wasn't conducive to his revenge plans. He'd only agreed to placate Leonard anyway. Letting the US Marshal have his way sometimes was the smart move.

"I wasn't aware we had a meeting tonight." Erik wiped his sticky mouth with a napkin.

"We didn't." Leonard nodded at Sarah as she poured him a cup. "Sarah, how are you this evening?"

She set a hand on her hip. "He ordered the pancakes."

"That's why I'm here."

"Still keeping an eye on him then?"

"When I can."

She sighed then narrowed her eyes a little. "You eating?"

"Nope."

She nodded then turned to Erik. "Done, Sugar?"

Erik pushed away his half-eaten stack of pancakes. "Yeah. And even if I wasn't, I'm sure I'd lose my appetite after the ass chewing I'm likely to receive."

"A deserved one, I'm sure." Shaking her head, she grabbed his plate then shuffled back behind the counter.

"She worries about you, kid."

"Not a kid."

Leonard grunted before sipping his coffee.

Even with Pavel's words pounding through his head, *"Never break first,"* Erik couldn't stem his inquiry. "What the hell does my eating pancakes have to do with anything?"

Leonard placed his hat on the table and then met his gaze. "You only eat them when you're troubled. I've mentioned this before."

"Pancake psychology, really? You go to college for that?"

"Sure did."

"Maybe I just wanted pancakes."

"Maybe."

Erik folded his hands together on top of the table. "What can I do for you tonight, Marshal?"

"Are you aware that Prince Khaled funded covert operations in Syria? Anyone meeting with him is instantly suspect and rightly so as a good chunk of his funds finance extremist factions."

"Don't see how this is relevant to me." Erik leaned back against the booth. "Other than he owns primary shares in National Trust, and I'm considering transferring funds."

"I'm sure a *funds* transfer will occur and that's why I'm here, kid. I've done what I can, but if you do business with that man, I'm finished."

Erik waited a beat to answer because the thought of disappointing Leonard churned his stomach. Nicki had suggested a Plan B, and he had one. He wasn't set to meet with Khaled until tomorrow, and the fact that Leonard knew shouldn't really surprise him. He respected this man, but had known all along he'd go too far one day and their sharing-just-enough-info-to-somewhat-trust-each-other relationship would end. "From the very beginning, you've known my intent. My purpose."

"And I've known you're a fool. Stop this now, kid. Go live a different life. Let the past go."

Erik gripped the sides of the table. "I made a vow."

"No." Leonard shook his head. "What you did was put up a wall. A barrier so the only thing you had to feel was revenge."

"Works for me."

"I'd hoped that after meeting Rachel, you'd see that your life could be different. That you could have family again."

"Rachel's better off without me."

"You've made sure of that."

"Yeah, I have." Erik took a deep breath. "And come to think of it, so are you, old man."

"So that's the way of it, is it?" Leonard gripped his coffee cup. "I know you're close to an end. I know you're forging alliances with some very nasty people. You're going down a road you can't ever walk away from. You think ruining Korzakov will bring about some kind of absolution, but it won't. This path you're taking will turn you into him."

Erik narrowed his eyes. "I'll never be him."

"You already are."

Erik slammed a fist against the table. "You need to leave."

Leonard remained where he was for a moment, before he grabbed his hat off the table and scooted out of the booth. He stood by the side of the table. "I've let a lot slide with you, kid, and that's something I'm not ashamed to say keeps me up at night. But you meet with that Saudi prince tomorrow, and I'll do everything in my power to put you away for life. Before I went into law enforcement, I fought in the first Gulf War, and I watched people die. Friends. Men I loved. You aren't the only one who's lost someone, but not everyone wastes their life seeking revenge. I've done what I can to make the world a better place. I've tried with you, but this is the last straw. After all our years working together, you've finally done what you've set out to do and turned me against you. And damned if you didn't break my heart a little in the process. Think about that before you meet with Khaled, Pavel. Think about that."

Erik's heart pounded and everything in him told him to stand and not let Leonard walk away. He didn't need this man as an enemy.

But he'd known how everything would end. That he'd stand alone against Korzakov and likely die in the process. Better to cut ties now. He'd rather no one mourned his loss anyway. And if he did survive. If his plan did work then Leonard was right in a way. He'd become something else. He'd owe a lot of people a lot of favors and Leonard couldn't be with him as he traveled down that road. No one could.

So, he said nothing as Leonard walked away.

Erik stepped out of the booth and tossed some money on the table. This had to be the last time. He couldn't come back here. His very presence revealed too much.

He rounded the counter and hugged Sarah. She smelled like coffee and cigarettes with a hint of maple syrup. Her soft graying hair, brushed against his cheek.

She stiffened before relaxing. "What's this?"

"Just thanking you for the meal."

She eased back in his arms. "Don't you do that to me, boy. You don't get to say goodbye." Her eyes watered a little and she sniffed before yanking a few napkins from a metal dispenser on the counter.

"Who says I'm saying goodbye?"

She turned and punched his shoulder. "Whatever it is, Erik, whatever you've done that has Marshal Moore leaving with a face like that, don't do it. I've made mistakes, and I've got so many regrets. You think I want to be here working my feet to the bone night after night. Life's about choices, and I haven't made good ones. Don't mess up your life. Be better, you hear me?"

"Yes." He hugged her again. "Katya always liked you. Said she wished she could've had a mom like you."

"Then she was an idiot, too. I had two kids and I fucked 'em up. Would've done the same to her. I ain't never been good for nobody. And if I was young like you, oh the changes I'd make. Different choices. Different life. So, if you really mean to say goodbye, if that's what this is, then hear me when I say, make the right choices."

"I am."

"No. You're not, you stubborn son of a bitch."

Erik kissed her wrinkled cheek. "I'll see you around."

She shook her head. "Katya loved you, Erik. I could see it in her eyes, and in every smile she ever gave you. And I can promise you that when a woman loves you that much, they only want the best for you. Are you doing that? Would she be proud of you right now?"

"She would understand." His mother was a fighter and that's what she'd expect him to do. Fight.

"No, she wanted you away from that life. I know this because she asked me to take you away. She had two hundred dollars in her little hand and she begged me to just take you." Sarah closed her eyes and a tear dripped from the corner of her eye. She wiped her nose and then met his gaze again. "I said no, and I'm sorry for that. I was scared. I knew who she belonged to, and I just couldn't. But I've regretted that moment ever since. Once again, I made the wrong choice and now you're saying goodbye—Oh, don't think I don't know a goodbye when I see one."

"Sarah, it's okay. Really it is." Erik grasped her frail shoulders. "I wouldn't have gone with you. I would've fought tooth and nail. I'm where I'm supposed to be."

"No, and that's the sad thing. You're not. You don't belong in places like this."

Erik cupped Sarah's cheek. "If I don't then neither do you."

Sarah pushed him away. "That's enough sap for one night. Get out of here and while you're at it, pull your head out of your ass and listen to Leonard. He knows what's best."

"Yeah, he does, but what works in his world doesn't work in mine."

Sarah patted his arm then walked off toward the women's restroom.

She didn't understand. Not really. And neither did Leonard. Revenge was all he had. All he knew. He huffed out a sigh and headed for his car.

A redheaded man was leaning against the trunk.

McCord.

"Finally showing up for work?" Erik pulled the .45 from his shoulder holster and racked the slide. McCord hadn't showed earlier when Erik completed a job for Korzakov, so why was he here now? "I hope you didn't scratch the paint."

In dark jeans and a black T-shirt, McCord straightened and trailed his fingers across the trunk of Erik's Bentley. "Nice car. Would be a shame if someone stole it then beat the shit out of it."

"I assume that's a reference to your own beating." If he'd known McCord planned to touch his Bentley, he would've brought his Monte Carlo instead. "If you're planning retribution of some sort, please let me know so I can just shoot you and get this over with."

"Nah." McCord planted both hands in his front pockets and rocked back on his heels. "That'd be too easy. Just wanted you to know, I have my eye on you, Pavel."

"Well, we are forced to work together, so...not like that's breaking news."

"You meet with cops often?" McCord jerked his head toward the diner.

"All the time." Erik grinned, because again his prior involvement with the US Marshals wasn't news.

McCord grunted, whether in agreement or just clearing his throat, Erik had no idea.

"I came here tonight, off the clock, as it were, to let you know how badly you've messed up." McCord shrugged a shoulder. "I only wanted one thing. The one thing I deserve. Jenny is my daughter, and I wanted to see her. That's all."

"You're delusional if you think that's all you'd do." Erik tightened his grip on the .45.

"We'll agree to disagree on my...shall we say...predilections." McCord chuckled. "Jenny is mine."

"You're demented." Erik's stomach churned. Good thing this man had been in prison for fifteen years. Children everywhere were much safer with this man behind bars.

"I am not demented." McCord fisted his hands at his sides. "Sexual relations between adults and children have always existed throughout history. My sexual orientation is the same as anyone else's. I'm no different than you."

Erik fought down a shudder, because out of all the disgusting people he'd dealt with over the years, he firmly believed McCord was the sickest. "I should've finished you at the warehouse." He kept his voice low. Security cameras were everywhere these days.

"And that's what this visit's about. I only wanted what is rightfully mine. And in the next couple months, as everything falls apart around you, I suggest you remember that."

"Are you threatening me?"

"Yes."

"I find I'm amused by that notion, as I could kill you right now."

"You won't and you want to know why?"

"Enlighten me."

"You strut around with your revenge plans, constructing this intricate web and you think you're ruthless. But as you say, you can just as easily put a bullet in me, but you don't. You plot and you plan. And now, I'm doing the same. I'll see you bloody and trapped as everything you've ever cared about is destroyed."

"Nice thought, but I don't care about anything or anyone." Erik shrugged, but an unwelcome slither of worry slid down his spine.

"Now, now, Pavel. We both know that's a lie. But since you've thrown down the gauntlet, I'll let you discover the falsehood in your declaration." McCord tsked out the side of his mouth and shot Erik a "finger gun" before striding down the alley and disappearing around the corner.

All Erik wanted was a stack of pancakes, instead he'd pissed off a US Marshal, upset a woman who was like a grandmother to him, and been served a side of crazy. And the most frightening realization of all was that McCord was right. Erik did have people he cared about, and he never should've let that happen.

He glanced back at the diner. Choices. Hadn't Sarah said that was what life was all about, and hadn't he already made his? He'd made a vow the day his mother was murdered, and he'd see it through to the end. McCord and his promises of retribution would have to wait, because if Erik knew anything about crazy—and he did—then he understood the man's threats were very real. They'd both had someone important ripped from their lives, and they'd both fight to see that rectified. In the end, Erik's choices weren't any better than McCord's. And that knowledge was a heady side dish that, no matter how it was served, wouldn't go down easy.

CHAPTER EIGHT

"Our agreement was for you to bring me information *before* it happens." Korzakov glared at the brown-skinned man sitting across from him.

A couple of traffic cops had grabbed his informant under the guise of a broken taillight, courtesy of Yegor, and now they were in this police interrogation room that smelled like sweat and lies. Korzakov generally preferred a more private locale to express his displeasure, but as dicey as the current situation was, he couldn't risk alerting anyone to his inside man.

"My supply lines suddenly halted." Korzakov glanced at the double-sided mirror. Cops were likely listening on the other side so he'd be very careful with his words. "Then one of my...shipments to Canada was seized by border patrol. Do you have any idea how much money I've lost this week?" He shoved the table against the man's chest.

The informant lifted a dark brow and steely-brown eyes met his gaze. "I'll say again, I left a message with your man, if he didn't pass it along, that's not my problem, you hear?"

"Oh, that's quite clever. Never been used before. Divide and conquer, is that your game?" Korzakov rolled his eyes. "Georgy is loyal to me. He says he heard nothing, therefore you sent nothing."

"I'd check with him again."

Korzakov slammed his hand against the steel tabletop. "Enough of this. Do what I'm paying you to do. Or instead of your family crossing the border, they'll die in creative and painful ways."

The man shifted forward in his chair, bound by the handcuffs behind his back. "Where's your boy, Georgy now? Check his messages. *I* didn't mess this up."

Korzakov stood from the table and tugged on his tie. "I want a report in two days. If not, I'll have your spic-ass brought in here again, and it won't be because of any traffic violation." He ran a finger over man's tattoo-covered arm. "I think they'd love you in prison. They'd love that virgin hole."

Raul threw back his head and laughed. "Next time you see me, I'll expect an apology. That lug of yours doesn't know how to work a phone. Bad business, Korzakov. Bad business."

He knocked on the door. "Let me out." His association with the man left a bad taste in his mouth.

After handing over a payout to the two cops who'd pulled over Raul, Korzakov texted Yegor to meet him at the police station's entrance. Making his way through the dregs of society, he nodded at the burly woman standing guard just inside the main doors before she pressed the button to allow his release. Leaving behind the smell of bad coffee and fear, he slipped outside and inhaled the fresh air.

He caught sight of Yegor and darted down the steps toward his Land Rover.

Yegor held open the back door.

"I'd like to speak to Georgy when we get to the office."

"Which office, sir?"

"Have him come to the lumberyard."

Yegor sucked in a breath. "What has my brother done?"

"Nothing. I only want to talk to him."

"But...the lumber house is...it's where we..."

"Not today." He patted Yegor's shoulder. "Do you know...does he keep his phone with him at all times?"

"Yes, just as you directed."

"And is he doing well, would you say?"

"Yes, he is well."

"Good." Korzakov nodded. "That's good. Tell him to meet us there and to bring his phone. I'm worried it's not working properly."

"Yes, sir." Yegor swallowed hard.

Korzakov settled into the back seat and checked his messages as Yegor pulled away from the curb. He'd hate to have to kill the man's brother. Plus Georgy had been with him since he was a child, but if the man couldn't relay a simple message then something had to be done. He'd lost millions this week.

The money could be made again, but the power he'd lost was immeasurable. He couldn't appear weak, or more than Erik Pavel and Frankie Castillo would begin to circle and snarl like a pack of ravaging wolves. Even though nothing could be tied back to either man, Korzakov knew they were behind his recent run of bad luck. He'd bide his time, and let the game play out before he made his move. When he did, he'd barely bat an eye at the blood pouring through the streets.

CHAPTER NINE

"What the hell, McCord." Erik yanked the man's arm away from the screaming woman, and shoved him against the industrial-sized freezer door.

"She called me a fag."

"And you take offence to *that?*"

Midday at a downtown high-end restaurant, they were collecting from the owner who was heavily in debt to Korzakov. Erik hated this kind of work, and that's why Korzakov sent him on these jobs.

Erik shifted to brace his forearm under McCord's neck. "We are here to give her a message, not to—"

"I was giving her one." Spittle flew from McCord's lips.

"Do not interrupt me when I'm speaking." Erik punched McCord's ribs.

The man gasped and turned a little green so Erik released him. He would *not* be vomited on.

The man dropped to his knees. "You'll pay for that."

Erik turned to the woman still ranting in Russian and told her to shut up in the same language before acknowledging McCord. "Go out to the car and wait for me. I'll finish in here."

McCord shot him a glare and then scrambled to his feet, cradling his arm against his side. "You're making it worse for yourself."

Erik narrowed his eyes. "I believe I said go out to the car. I did not say you could speak to me."

McCord's nostrils flared and he stood his ground for a moment before he kicked open the employee door and stepped outside.

Erik's entire body vibrated with the need to destroy. He clenched his jaw, breathed deeply, and then rubbed his temples before facing the restaurant manager, Stella—according to her nametag. "Come here."

The older woman with high cheekbones, who couldn't weigh more than a hundred pounds, whimpered and shook her head. Her hand was pressed against her cheek, which had a slight pink tinge from McCord's slap.

Patience had never been a virtue, and this whole scene brought forth far too many memories. The smell of fish was pervasive. Why even serve fish in Ohio unless it was freshwater? How fresh could seafood actually be in the Midwest?

Erik swallowed hard to keep from gagging. He'd been in this moment far too many times with his makeshift father, Pavel. Only that monster would've done much worse than McCord. He'd have beat this woman bloody and then thrown her in the freezer. "I said, come here. I won't ask again."

Stella shuffled over, mumbling choice curse words in Russian.

"I understand everything you are saying, and I'll ask that you just be quiet for a moment so I can complete my task." He glanced at the woman's downturned head and sighed again. "Look at me when I speak to you."

She met his gaze with a whole lot of attitude shining in her eyes.

"Good." Erik shoved both hands in his pockets. "The owner of this restaurant is a complete and utter fool. I commend your loyalty to him. However, he obtained a loan from the wrong person. And when he doesn't pay one way, you can bet he'll pay another. I know you understand this." He pinched her chin between his thumb and index finger.

She flinched and jerked away.

God this place reeked.

And he was sweating. Why was he sweating?

He couldn't do this anymore.

He was better than this. And this woman shouldn't have to pay for her owner's bad decision. The road to this realization was long. For many years, he'd stood alongside Pavel and had been a good son—an obedient son. As a teen, he'd have had no qualms about making this woman a bruised and bloody message, because if he hadn't, he'd have received a beating of his own back home for disobeying or appearing weak in front of Pavel's men.

"Listen lady, just tell your boss to pay, and find someplace else to work, because the next people who'll come collect won't be as nice. They'll—Oh my God. What is that smell?"

With a small cry, she jumped back.

"No wonder you don't have any money if your place reeks like this." He cupped a hand over his nose. "Get your fish overnighted, lady. And no tilapia. Do you even know where that fish comes from?"

"I'm sorry. "

He flicked a hand toward her office. "Go get the money. I'll wait outside for two minutes, and if you don't come out, I'll send McCord back in." He wouldn't, but she didn't know that. He was done with McCord. Done with Korzakov. Castillo's plans were moving forward. So why was he even here?

"I'll be right back." Stella waved a finger then hustled off.

Erik headed outside, tugging on his tie. Once outside, he squinted against sun's bright glare. He blinked then braced his hands on both knees and took a cleansing breath.

So this was it. His very last job for Korzakov. He felt no joy, no peace, but why should he? He was still locked in this world. Still trapped in this maze of deceit and lies.

Throughout all his scheming, he frequently wondered what

Pavel would think of his plans. His stand-in father wouldn't care that his motive was revenge for Katya's death, he'd just be proud Erik was destroying Korzakov. That thought had made him pause a few times. But when he'd started this path, he'd known at the end, once Korzakov fell, he'd fall, too.

———

A FEW HOURS later with his heart pounding steadily in his chest, Erik sat in a metal folding chair, which was set before a desk covered in papers and someone's leftover lunch. A fly landed in a blob of ketchup. The buzz of panel and table saws, poured into the office from the lumberyard. Having deadly blades just outside the door wasn't the greatest place to end his agreement with Korzakov.

Erik had called the mafia leader for a meeting after leaving the restaurant—and McCord. He'd also left a message with Castillo about his plans. After Leonard's visit, he'd put off meeting with Khaled, but after today, he had no other choice. He needed the prince's backing on a global scale. For an empire to fall, he needed another empire to take over. And Khaled had an even bigger presence in the underworld than Korzakov or Castillo.

Erik straightened in his seat and met Korzakov's gaze. "I'm done working with McCord. I know he was only placed with me because you believe I give a shit about Sheridan Bennett."

Korzakov sank back in his chair. Georgy stood behind him. The burly man had a red mark on his cheek as if someone had recently punched him. Erik glanced down and saw a smashed cell phone on the floor. "What's up, Georgy? Why the long face? Isn't that your phone on the floor?"

Georgy and Korzakov exchanged a glance. Then the big man came around the desk, picked up his phone, and dropped it in a metal garbage can.

The loud bang reverberated around the room.

"You plan to kill him then." Korzakov rested his elbows on the desk.

"Who Georgy?" Erik snapped his gaze back to Korzakov. "Why? What did he do?"

Yegor stepped inside the room, shoving the door hard enough it slammed against the inner wall. "What was that sound?"

Erik looked back and forth between the two brothers, something wasn't quite right here. What had he interrupted?

"Nothing to worry over, Yegor. Your brother dropped his phone in the garbage."

Yegor glanced at his brother then glared at Korzakov.

Erik arched a brow.

Korzakov cleared his throat. "Yegor, take your brother out of the room. I'm done with him."

"Done with him?" Well now, wasn't this interesting. "Are your *boys* giving you trouble then?"

Yegor halted in his stride then growled out something in Russian.

"I'm done *speaking* to him." Korzakov flicked his fingers at Yegor. "You two wait outside the door." He waited for them to leave before facing Erik again. "Do you know if it's possible to plant a message on someone's phone at a later date?"

"What?" Erik furrowed his brow. "Why?"

"Nothing." Korzakov sniffed then opened a couple desk drawers, producing a bottle of Blanton's and a glass. "You were saying you plan to kill McCord."

"I didn't say that. His death is your call, not mine."

"You're right." Korzakov swirled the freshly-poured glass of bourbon in his hand.

Without being excused, Erik stood and brushed at his lapel. "The decisions and choices you've made carry consequences."

"So, you're doing this, are you?" Korzakov sat forward in his seat. "Don't think I don't know who is behind the slight...issues I've had this week, but I'll let you continue your little revenge plot as it amuses me to watch you flail about."

Erik shoved his hands in his pockets so he didn't leap across the table and choke the old man. "Eight years ago, I stood quiet and still as you took my mother from me. She was my everything, and now, I'm taking everything from you."

"You can try." Korzakov shrugged.

"You said I wasn't a man, that I was weak, and that I needed a lesson in how to survive in your brutal world. Then you pulled that trigger. You left her on the cold floor, blood pouring from her chest." Fury rising, Erik narrowed his eyes. "I'm the one holding the gun now."

"Do your worst, Pavel. Others have tried before."

"I don't have to *try* anything." Erik pasted on a smile and hoped he was the only one who could hear his thudding heartbeat. "It's already done."

"Ah...my blood is pumping, I must say. You are a formidable one, but then I've made you what you are. It'll be like fighting myself. I can't wait."

Erik tipped his chin in acknowledgement. "I'll see you in hell, Korzakov."

Korzakov slanted his glass in Erik's direction. "I believe Yegor and Georgy would like a say in this conversation."

"Based on the looks Yegor was casting your way, I don't think he's your biggest fan right now."

"He's a bit overprotective of his brother. As you know, family is a weakness. Family like, your sister Rachel...or Nicki...where should we put her in your spectrum?"

Erik stilled by the door. "I watched one woman die by your hand, I'll not have another."

"You've just threatened me. How do you expect I'll react? Not to mention these tricks you've played this week." He shook his head. "Erik, Erik, Erik, once again, you've brought this upon yourself." He glanced at the door. "Yegor! Get in here!"

Erik widened his stance and waited for the big guy to storm

through the door, but nothing happened. "Guess you shouldn't have hit his brother."

Korzakov threw his glass against the door. "Get out."

Erik took a final look at the man behind the desk. "Each brick will fall and once that wall is gone, I'll be standing on the other side. I'll put a bullet in your chest and walk away. Enjoy this moment of peace, it's the last one you'll have."

Erik sidestepped to the door, opened it, and then glanced around quickly, searching for Yegor. Not detecting anyone, Erik breathed a sigh of relief before dashing down the stairwell and exiting the building.

In the parking lot, he stilled upon hearing a door slam open.

Yegor shouted in Russian to someone, likely Georgy.

Erik jogged over to his car, pressing the trunk button on his key fob.

Footsteps pounded on the pavement.

Five more steps and he'd make it to his car. Yegor had searched him before entering Korzakov's office, something he'd known would occur, so he didn't have a weapon...but he kept plenty in the trunk.

"Where you going in such a hurry, Erik?" Yegor called from just behind him.

Georgy grabbed Erik's arm.

Erik whipped around, lifting his elbow and spinning with enough force to crack Georgy in the jaw.

Breaking away, Erik shoved open his trunk and grabbed his .45.

Yegor barreled forward, knocking him against the back end of his Bentley and almost shoving him into the open trunk.

Erik delivered two quick jabs to Yegor's ribs.

The man released him and stepped back, pressing a hand against his side.

A delivery van barreled around the corner and screeched to a halt inches from where Yegor stood.

The driver's door opened and Raul, one of Castillo's men climbed out.

"Pavel. What's up?" Raul slapped a metal pipe against his palm. "These boys bothering you?"

Yegor frowned. "Taking sides are you, Raul? The boss will be very interested in hearing this."

"Have you always been a snitch?" Raul pointed the end of the pipe at Yegor. "I was just driving by and thought I'd even the odds. Plus, I need a good fight every once in a while. Spilled blood gets my dick hard."

Georgy cracked his knuckles. "Drop the weapon first."

"Oh, no. You should know by now, I don't fight fair." Raul charged forward, lifting the pipe above his head.

Georgy and Yegor both roared and attacked Raul.

Erik stood back and watched it unfold.

Raul busted Georgy in the jaw with the pipe then slid to his knees and whacked Yegor in the knee. The big guy went down, and Raul shot to his feet and bashed him on the back of the head.

Georgy shot forward, but Raul punched him right in the windpipe.

Georgy clutched his throat, gasping for air before he dropped to the ground.

Chest heaving, Raul turned and slapped Erik on the back. "Buy me dinner, Pavel. I'm thinking a big steak."

Erik blinked. "What? How did you even know to come here?"

"Castillo asked me to drive by."

"I see." Yet something didn't quite add up. Why would Castillo only send one man? Erik glanced up at Korzakov's office then down at the moaning defeated Russians. Maybe Raul *was* the only man needed for the job, and he wanted to eat after this? *What the hell?*

Plus, Erik wasn't safe to be around. They needed to vacate immediately, and park it for the night at a safe house. Erik had to warn Rachel and Nicki. And on top of that, most people who worked at this lumberyard were under Korzakov's thumb, and he didn't want to wait for a round two, which would likely involve some kind of automatic rifle.

"You need to get back to Castillo, Raul. Thank you for this, but go now." Everything Erik had worked for was falling into place, and first blood had been spilled. Seeking to steady his nerves, he turned and shut the car's trunk, ignoring the slight shake in his hands.

Yegor groaned.

Raul kicked him in the side then turned back to Erik. "Korzakov will retaliate for this."

Erik opened his driver's side door. "I'm ready."

"Are you? He'll hit hard...these men...they do unspeakable things to each other for nothing more than money and power."

Erik spared a glance at the tattooed man. "And here I thought your boss, Castillo hated Korzakov because of what he did to Carlos?"

"Are you referring to Frankie's half-brother?"

"Yes."

Korzakov was rumored to be responsible for Carlos's career-ending injury in a mixed-martial arts match. Years before the fight took place, Carlos had walked away from Frankie and the mafia life to become a MMA fighter. Carlos was set to fight against a man who owed Korzakov a heavy financial debt. Korzakov had used the opportunity to allow the man to repay his debt and to express his anger over a drug contract Castillo had bid on and won. During the bout, the man in debt had locked Carlos in a knee bar and hadn't released him even though Carlos was tapping-out. The knee injury ruined Carlos's career, and everyone knew the injury hadn't been accidental.

"You can believe Castillo is only in this life for Carlos and his family if you want." Raul took three steps toward his van before stopping and speaking over his shoulder. "But then you'd be a fool."

Erik watched the man leave then hopped into his car and raced out of the parking lot. What kind of message was Raul trying to send? Not a puzzle he had time to work out, especially now that he had a bright red target on his back.

CHAPTER TEN

Nicki balanced her to-go cup in one hand, her takeout sandwich bag in the other, and tried to open her apartment door without spilling everything. Today had been a doozy. She'd had two no-shows and had to break up a cat fight between two stylists over some guy they'd met the weekend before who'd been texting them both. The whole day was ridiculous, but she wouldn't trade all that craziness for anything. She'd been through worse. A few scratches from girls who had no idea how to fight were nothing.

Eagerly anticipating her grilled chicken Panini, she eased into her apartment and toed off her heels. A bit of dinner then reading while drinking a cup of herbal tea would do nicely.

"Hello, Nicki."

She shrieked and jostled her Sprite, catching the cup before it fell onto her new entry rug. "What in the world?" Pressing a hand against her racing heart, she glared at Erik, sitting like some kind of psycho-stalker in her living room. No lights. No warning. And certainly no key. "How did you get in here—You know what? Never mind. Get out. I had a not-so-nice day, and I want to eat my dinner and chill. Not deal with whatever craziness you've got happening today."

"You no longer have a choice. Come in and sit down."

"I always have a choice. And I'll sit down because my feet hurt and I'm hungry, not because I'm obeying you."

He tapped a finger against his chin. Once again, the man looked amazing in his black suit, with a green tie this time.

"I've decided to come clean since that's the only way I can keep you safe." Erik ran a hand through his already ruffled hair. "I started something earlier that's placed you in the line of fire. Something you'll not be able to deny, nor will I let you."

Nicki took a long drink from her bubbly soda. Everything was so doom and gloom with this man. "Can I just finish my dinner before you tell me my life is over?"

"Actually, I'd prefer you to pack a bag and then you can eat on the way to your new location."

Her jaw dropped. "My new location. Seriously?"

"Very."

She sighed before dropping her dinner on the coffee table. "Just tell me."

"We need to move first."

Was this a ploy to get her to Vegas? This man was manipulation personified. She narrowed her eyes and slid her straw back and forth in the plastic lid. "I've been at work all day. I'm here now. If something bad was going to happen, why hasn't it already?"

"It will."

"Lovely." She flopped onto her green couch.

"Go get packed."

She opened her mouth to argue, but something in his tone sent a chill down her spine. "Whatever." She stood and headed to her bedroom. "But as I'm packing, you're talking, because I need to have an idea of how long I'll be gone."

Erik followed her into the bedroom. "All right."

His easy agreement worried her further. She looked over her shoulder and raised a brow.

"Fine, in a nut shell, I've declared war on Korzakov. I've allied with Frankie Castillo. Frankie wants you in Vegas, so that's where we're going."

Nicki stilled with a grouping of socks in her hands. "Frankie Castillo, are you out of your mind?"

"We both want the same thing."

She threw the socks on her bed and faced Erik. "Oh, he wants *things* all right. You'll owe him forever. You know that, right?"

"What's done is done."

After releasing a few choice words about his stupidity, she punched his arm. "Do you know what he did to the guy that handicapped his brother?"

"Technically it was his half-brother."

She held back a scream but a shriek came out anyway. "Castillo is known for 'the stew' or *el guiso*. He douses his victims in gasoline then burns them alive in oil barrels. What the hell, Pavel? Castillo's evil tactics are even worse than the time my mom's second husband took me out fishing, and when I wouldn't suck him off, he tossed me in the lake and told me to swim for it."

Erik leaned against the wall, crossing both arms over his chest. "Really, well that's almost as bad as the time Pavel made me watch as he placed his broker's head in an industrial vice and kept pressing down until the man's eyes popped out of his head."

Nicki growled and stomped her foot. "This whole thing"—she waved her arms wildly—"isn't a game anymore. Everything I've told you, everything I've ever said is the truth. I don't want to see you burned alive in a barrel or dumped in a lake. What is the matter with you!"

"Do you think *I've* been lying when we have these conversations?"

"I didn't live through all my bullshit to die because of you." Dang it! She would not cry. She wasn't a hopeless lost female anymore. She was strong. Independent. A survivor.

"And you won't die, Nicki, if you just listen to me."

"Frankie Castillo, Erik. El guiso!"

Erik sucked in lips then released them with a pop. "Yeah."

Nicki did scream this time then stomped to her closet and hauled out her suitcase. "You're insane. I knew this. I *so* knew this, so why I keep getting surprised, I'll never know. And why I'm not getting in my car right now and going to the police, I'll never know either."

"*I* know."

"Oh? Care to enlighten me?"

"The cops are paid off...by Castillo and Korzakov or both."

"I'm so sick of that generalization. Not all cops are bad. I've had a few help me over the years."

"I'm sure you have."

"Don't placate me, Pavel."

"Wasn't aware I was."

"How long?"

"What?"

Instead of stabbing his eye out for saying, "what" again, she braced her fisted hands on her hips. "How long are we planning on being in Vegas with Frankie-fucking-Castillo?"

He stared at her for a moment then grabbed her shoulders and crept forward until they were backed up against her dresser. "Listen. I know you didn't ask for this. I know you thought you'd escaped this life, and I promise you that once I'm done, you'll be done. Even if it takes my life, I'll do that for you. All the pieces of Korzakov are falling down, and I'll make sure you're not caught in the debris."

She breathed heavily, irritated by his closeness yet at the same time the danger oozing out of his pores did something to her. The whole bad-boy persona apparently flipped her switch, which was stupid...and oh, so very hot.

He stared at her lips.

She wet them with a quick swipe of her tongue. Heat and chemistry and that dangerous edge had always existed between them. The element of danger, the hope to tame, something so forbidden, every piece of it was there, calling to her. She knew how to please a man. Knew she could please this one, and she'd love to watch him break.

But he stepped back.

No! Not this time. She gripped the back of his neck and drew him down, kissing him hard and dirty and wet. She slid her free hand down his chest to his thick and very hard cock then cupped his soft sacs and squeezed.

He gasped into her mouth.

With a satisfied grin, Nicki bit his bottom lip and tugged. "You think you can come in here and rearrange my life? You think *you* are in charge? No, I don't think so." She nipped his chin. "There's a price to everything, Erik, and you're paying it, right now. Get on the bed."

"We don't have time—"

"I said, get on the bed."

Without a word, he lowered onto the side of the bed.

A taste after waiting so long—that's all she wanted, well that and for him to beg. Kneeling before him, she undid his belt.

He tried to grip her hair and bring her up for another kiss, but she shook him off. "I didn't say you could touch me."

"Wait. Why, are you doing this, Nicki?"

"Because I want to. Have for a while. Figure you'll probably die soon, so this is my last chance."

"No, that isn't why." He gripped her shoulders and gave her a little shake.

She looked into his eyes and no longer saw lust but confusion and maybe...pity? "Let go of me."

"Tell me, why?"

She struggled in his grasp.

"Say it. Say you like the power. The control. You like bringing men to their knees."

"Fuck you. I'm the one on my knees here, Pavel."

"You can't control everything with sex."

"You sanctimonious asshole." She shook free and rose to her feet.

How dare he tell her how to solve problems? Him, who lived his life solving only one.

"Why, Nicki? Enlighten me."

She couldn't say a word, because he was right. She'd gotten scared and sought solace in sex. Sought control in an arena where she felt strong. But damn him for saying so.

"God." Erik blew out a long breath. "We are both so fucked up about what love and sex and relationships are supposed to be. And that is exactly why I don't do any of them."

She barked out a laugh, pacing in front of him. "You don't have sex? Sorry, don't believe you."

"Nicki." He tried to grab her hand, but she slapped him away. "The point is you're an intelligent, successful woman. Not only do we not have time for whatever this is, but I won't let you use me so you can get off on some power trip."

"All right. You can shut the hell up now, because you've made your point. You think you know me so well, how about you turn that all-knowing gaze inward sometime. Maybe then you'd forgive a girl for trying to get a little of her own back." Her voice had risen in level as she spoke to the point she was likely yelling loud enough for her neighbors to hear. "I have no idea why I even bother with you. You're like the dog that keeps barking and growling, but I try to pet it anyway, so why am I surprised when you bite?"

"I have no idea."

"Don't agree with me, you asshole. And get the hell out of my face, will ya?"

He shook his head. "Pack."

"You basically just called me a power-tripping whore and now you want me to go to Vegas with you? Are you trying to make me insane?"

"*I* don't want you to go anywhere with me. Castillo does."

"Oh, well then, of course. Let's go right now." She headed toward her bedroom door, because fuck him, fuck packing, and fuck the last fifteen minutes of her jacked-up life.

"It's Castillo's daughter's birthday."

"How freaking lovely for her."

"Her twenty-first birthday."

Stopping in the doorway, Nicki had visions of shot glasses filled with tequila lined up on the bar before some guy in a Punisher T-shirt showed up with an automatic rifle and killed everyone. "Have you gotten El guiso's daughter a present yet?"

"A present?"

"This should be good. Maybe even worth going to Vegas to see." She headed into the bathroom, keeping her mouth running with mumbled curses so she didn't cry or scream, or who even knew what at this moment.

"And what's worth seeing?"

The man had the audacity to grab her shoulder.

With narrowed eyes, she glanced at his hand. "Get your filthy paw off of me. Let's just say I'll only go to Vegas to see you hanging from nothing but your balls off that Eiffel tower." She slammed the bathroom door in his face and turned on the shower. He was ranting on the other side but she'd heard enough from him tonight.

He'd been right to stop her. What had she been thinking? She *did* equate control with sex. She'd even said he was paying a price for trying to control her. Why had she slipped back into that old role?

Embarrassment heated her cheeks. Yet, Erik wasn't quite right about one thing. Her efforts weren't so much about control as wanting to be close to him, seeking comfort for her fears. Foolish. So very foolish. And yet her heart always seemed to want the ones that ripped her to pieces.

Her prison group had discussed moments like this, when everything around her seemed to crash and burn. They'd say to rise like a phoenix from the ashes, to brush off the old and welcome the new. To try to find her center again and focus.

How that would be possible when leaving one murderous crime boss and flying to another, was beyond her. And how she could face

Erik, knowing she'd once again offered him a piece of her only to be denied?

Feeling a bit of panic slither through her tired bones, she turned and stared into the mirror. "What happens in Vegas, stays in Vegas, and if I end up burned alive in some gas-filled barrel, I'm coming back and haunting Erik Pavel forever."

CHAPTER ELEVEN

Wow! Ostentatiousness much. Who spent this kind of money on a birthday party? The sparkling wine tower trickling into actual glasses, the five-tiered cake, and the famous Los Angeles DJ were all set up in a Vegas hotel's brightly lit ballroom. For a kid who'd been tossed a birthday card across the kitchen table on no more than two occasions, this party seemed ridiculous. But also kind of...nice. Castillo—psychopath though he was—obviously loved his daughter, and the twenty-one year old girl didn't seem like an entitled princess. Still, did she realize her father did horrible things in order to pay for this slightly-too-pink bash?

In order to keep her heart from being cut out and her dismembered-body dumped off a bridge, Nicki had gifted the girl with a package to the Beauty Bar.

Erik had remained by Nicki's side all night, which kind of annoyed her. This idea that he *had* to be close in order to protect her seemed ludicrous. He had Rachel and other sort-of friends. Wasn't he concerned about them? He hadn't answered any of her questions about his plans on the plane, so she'd texted Rachel instead, but hadn't received a response.

Sitting beside her at the round table, Erik nudged her shoulder. "Don't you want to hit the dance floor and do the 'Wobble?'"

"No." Nicki shifted her weight. These new black heels and this slinky black dress had been purchased by someone and delivered to her room. One did not dance in new heels and expect not to fall on their face. "I'm good. Thanks." She sipped her red wine, smiling as she imagined Erik Pavel actually doing the Wobble dance. "How much longer are we expected to stay?"

"Not much."

He looked dapper, as always, in a well-tailored black suit, topped with purple tie.

"I still haven't heard from Rachel. And even though you refuse to tell me anything, I'd like to know if she's okay? *I* happen to care about people."

"Clayton left a message about ten minutes ago that he was taking everyone out of town but wouldn't say where."

"Right, probably a good idea not to tell you, so when Korzakov has your balls strapped to an electric fence you can't scream the location."

"You're awfully worried about my balls, Nicki." Erik arched a dark brow and pressed against her side.

"Hardly."

Erik gripped her chin. "You can cut the attitude. I stopped you before we left because we didn't have time for that, and you were doing it for the wrong reasons."

"Blowjob, Pavel. I assume you're referencing the blowjob. No man ever stops a blowjob unless he's insane. And the vague referencing thing you're doing is super irritating. We're not twelve."

He trailed a finger against her bare arm. "You're sexy as fuck, but you know this. We'd burn so hot together, like the blue part of the flame. But you've been through enough in your life. Hurt enough. And I've got nothing to offer you but the same."

Fury and, a small twinge of lust, fired through her blood at his touch. He wasn't allowed to tell her what she wanted and who she was. Hell, she was still figuring that out for herself. "First off, don't get all handsy now. Second, I never said I wanted that white picket fence with a dog lolling around in the yard."

"And I'd never offer you that."

"Then we're clear." Nicki shook her head and laughed.

"What?"

"Men."

"I am, yes, last time I checked, although after this ridiculous conversation, I'll need to see if my dick's still attached."

She pressed a hand against his crotch and found him half-hard. "Yeah, you're good."

He hissed.

She grinned.

"We'll fuck...at some point. It's highly likely." He gripped her hand and locked her fingers with his.

After glancing around to be sure no one was listening, she lowered her voice. "We'll fuck? Oh, Erik. See that's why I laughed. A woman does have needs, and yes, if I wanted a man or a woman, it wouldn't be hard to find someone to fill that slot...literally. So don't act like you're something I need." She yanked away her hand. "I've tried with you over and over again, and after yesterday, why would I ever try again?"

He narrowed his eyes. "You'd just have sex with some random stranger? Thought you were done with that?"

"*That?* Meaning what? Sex?" She twisted in her chair and faced him fully. "Because I *know* you didn't mean sex for pay, because then I'd have to stab you with a fork. For your information, jackass, *I do* choose my partners now. *I* make the decision. *I'm* in control. Don't for one second say *you* are not the kind for one-nighters, 'cause I'll call you a liar. Man, you are such a judgmental asshole."

"Okay, okay." He held up a hand between them. "I'm sorry. I was out of line."

"Yeah, you were. Now, I'm getting up and leaving you behind because once again, you've managed to piss me off." She flashed a fake smile before walking away. Their conversations were supposed to be meaningless banter, and lately they'd teetered a little too close to all that remained unsaid and undone between them. But as he'd said, he had nothing to give, so why did she walk away every time wishing he did?

CLUTCHING the refilled red wine glass she'd obtained from the bar down the hall, Nicki stood just inside the doorway to Castillo's party. Dancers shimmied under the sparkling lights. A loud hip-hop tune thumped through the room. A squadron of men stood on the outskirts, dressed in black suits and looking for any signs of trouble. Nicki glanced at the smiling birthday girl. At twenty-one, Nicki was in love with Ariel and living as an escort. Oh, the things she wished she could whisper in that girl's ear, but she couldn't go back, and really had no desire to.

She sipped her wine. The semi-dry, slight-blackberry flavor burst across her tongue. She hadn't eaten anything from Castillo's party, because she couldn't digest something bought by illegal means. She'd decided to stand on some kind of moral high ground regardless of how small and petty her actions seemed.

Slipping into the room, she searched for Erik. Her feet were killing her, and the dangly diamond drop earrings made her ears itch. Basically, she wanted out of this dress—and this situation. Moments like this mirrored the life she used to live. Where she had to fake everything, smile at the right times, and make witty conversation.

Frankie Castillo maneuvered through the tables, heading in her direction.

She averted her gaze, pulling her phone from her purse.

He stopped at her side, his bodyguards halting just behind him. "Are you enjoying the party, Ms. Nobles?"

She grinned down at the shorter man before tucking away her phone. "Your daughter is very lovely."

He grinned. "Nicely done."

"I'm the queen of evasive answers. I'm sorry to say that your friend, Pavel is rubbing off on me."

"Is he not your friend, too?"

"No. I'm more like his...prisoner and since I've done the whole incarcerated thing before, I can't say I like doing it again."

"I see." Castillo waved a hand toward an empty table. "Come sit with me a moment."

Of course his request wasn't something she could refuse. She scanned the room for Erik again and caught his eye. She tried using mental mind powers to send a silent save-my-ass message. He probably figured she was either squinting or needed to sneeze. He really needed a course in interpreting facial expressions, because her covert-communicado had been *very* clear.

Castillo took her arm. "Over here looks good."

Trying not to sigh, Nicki stumbled along beside him and sat in the chair he'd pulled out for her. After placing her wine glass on the table, she cleared her throat. "Quite the party for your daughter. I was reminiscing on my own childhood earlier and couldn't help but compare."

Castillo settled beside her, close enough that their knees almost brushed together. "No clowns or balloon animals, I'm guessing?"

"Clowns?" She shivered. "Have you seen the movie *IT*? No thanks."

He chuckled. "I've actually read the book. Imagine that."

"Not hard to imagine."

"Is that so?" He narrowed his eyes. "You've made no assumptions? You disrespect me by not partaking of what I've provided yet you sit before me and imagine?"

Her heart began to race, but she simply shrugged a shoulder. "I stopped trying to please men a few years ago. Sorry."

He tapped his heavily tattooed finger against the table. "And Erik, are you pleasing him?"

She turned and met Castillo's dark gaze. "Although that's none of your business, I did say he and I aren't friends."

"You and Erik are both my business." He eased back in his chair. "What do you see when you look around this room?"

Nicki kept her gaze on Castillo, because his question wasn't really about what was happening around them. "I see a party for a young girl."

He studied her for a moment. "And what else?"

Taking a sip of her wine for fortification, she let the liquid settle on her tongue for a moment before swallowing. "I see a desire for the good life. In your clothes, in your pile of gifts, and in the glitter of this room. I see tattoos, and I know they hold various meanings. I see death and pain and too many ridiculous gold chains."

He barked out a laugh and murmured something in Spanish to the two men who sat behind her. They all laughed.

Surrounded by men who could slip a garrote around her neck made her twitchy. *What the hell is Erik doing?* Why wasn't he coming over after she'd given him the save-me eyes?

"Based on what I've learned about you, Nicki, I shouldn't be surprised that you don't see it."

"*It?* I thought we established no clowns were at this party?" She chuckled, because he'd turned serious all of a sudden and that freaked her the hell out.

"Family." Castillo waved a hand around the room. "That's what I see when I look around. I see *mi madre, mi padre, mi esposa, y mi hijo.* You may wonder why I do what I do, and I would say to you, it's all right here. Family, whether it's my real family or my *pandilla* family. Everything in this room is what matters."

She nodded, hoping they were getting to the point of this conversation.

"I had Erik bring you here because I don't trust a man with no family. Something's very wrong with a man who has no brothers, no mother, and no father, you follow me?"

"Actually I do." She knew all about not having a family, even more so than Erik, because his still existed. He still had a sister who cared—and parents, though they were estranged. Nicki had nothing. And the one woman whom she'd considered her only family and friend had sent her to jail. So yeah, she understood more than this man could ever know.

"And you, I know you have no family either."

She huffed out a laugh. "I don't. Not all of us need this."

He smiled and shook his head. *"This* is everything. *Family* is everything." He unbuttoned his shirt and pointed to a black hand tattoo on his chest. "This was my very first piece. We call it the black hand of death. All these tattoos are a symbol of who I am. They tell a story of what I've done and what I'm willing to do for my family."

Since he was covered in tattoos, he'd obviously do a lot. She knew this about him but refrained from going into specifics because dismemberment didn't really go with pinot noir.

"Mr. Castillo, not all of us have what you have." And she'd never really let herself dwell on her lack of a true family. Her life was what it was. Everyone who was supposed to love her had betrayed her in some way. Her mother beat her. Her father was an unknown entity. She had no siblings, so the concept of family was quite foreign, and not necessarily welcome. "Family is a fallacy made by TV shows and movies. Real life hurts and family doesn't always have your back."

"Ah." He held up a finger. "And that is my point, you *can* have family if you choose to." He stood and held out his hand.

Absolutely confused, she took his hand. Did he want her to go somewhere? Were they done talking? Why would he say she should choose to have a family? Hadn't he heard a word she'd said?

"Family is everything because family is blood." He patted her hand. "Offer this to Erik, and he'll give you everything."

She nodded, because she wasn't sure if she was supposed to give Erik family or give him blood. Neither really worked for her.

Castillo nodded then walked off with his men.

She sank into her seat and downed the rest of the wine, seriously considering going back and asking for an entire bottle. Thinking about her past, her abusive mother, the fact that she'd never known her dad, and all the men in and out of her life both as a child and as a teen, plus Ariel's betrayal made her want to get absolutely drunk.

Survival. That was her code. The whole family thing might work for Castillo but not for her.

And the thought that she and Erik could form some kind of family?

What?

No.

Never.

She huffed out a laugh. Castillo, the homicidal cupid, could put away his arrows because she wasn't ever going to be a homemaker. But hey, kudos to all the women who did make family work. And cheers to women who were happy in that sphere. The whole idea of home and hearth scared her shitless because then she had something to lose, and hadn't she already lost enough?

She stared at her empty wine glass and considered why she felt so hollow. *Enough with the pity party, Nobles.*

Alcohol. And lots of it. The numbing agent of the ages. Plus, didn't it always make her feel better when she woke up the next day on the bathroom floor with her entire head on the verge of explosion? Hell, yes!

Leaving her sky-high heels under the table, she grabbed her wine glass and headed for the other bar, considering how much of a dent an entire bottle or two could make on her debit card.

CHAPTER TWELVE

After extracting himself from an impromptu poker game with Castillo, Erik finally took a moment to find Nicki. He'd texted her before the game started, and she'd replied she was at the bar down the hall.

As he walked in, he caught a glimpse of her shiny black hair and stopped to enjoy the view. Her back narrowed to a V in the open evening gown, revealing her smooth skin. Her hair was lifted in some intricate bun-braid thing that women created, which had wisps falling against her shoulders.

Her body, her mind, and that mouth tempted him all the time. For far too long they'd been look-but-don't-touch, but his cock filled when he thought of her taking him deep down her throat. He still didn't understand why he'd stopped her. Yet, her motives were all wrong. And did he really deserve Nicki when his whole life revolved around destroying another human being? Regardless of his more animalistic needs, he was well aware his vow of revenge would always take precedence. But if that were the case, then why was Nicki here? He could've refused Castillo's request and come alone.

He didn't obey orders, so that meant she was here because he'd made a choice, which was a very dangerous thing for this beauty.

He strolled up to her and placed a hand on her cool shoulder. "Nicki."

She turned and flashed a wide grin. "Hey, well lookie who's here, Mr. Judgmental Jerk-pants is up in the house. Whoop! Whoop!"

Oh boy.

He spied the half-empty wine bottle on the bar. "Drinking your cares away?"

"Yep." She lifted her glass in a mock toast before swallowing what was left. "And as you can see, they're all gone now."

"I brought your shoes." He dangled them before her then glanced at two of Castillo's men who sat at a table by the bar's door. Their presence was why she was unharmed. "How about we take the rest of that bottle up to the room?" He'd learned a long time ago to never suggest a woman needed to stop drinking...or anything else for that matter.

"Sure. Sure." She stood and gripped his arm. As she put her shoes back on, she wobbled a few times, but quickly righted herself with a booming laugh. "Let's go to the room. I think I need to lie down."

Erik waved down the bartender. "She good here?"

The man nodded. "Yeah, take care of that beauty." He smirked before grabbing her empty glass.

Frowning at the man, Erik turned and wrapped an arm around Nicki's slim shoulders and tried not to imagine her soft curves rising and falling with his body. He lifted the bottle between them while leading her to the elevators. "Why the whole bottle, Nicki?"

The elevator dinged.

They stepped inside.

She dug into her little purse, mumbling about the key.

He removed the card from his pocket and tapped the security bar on the elevator's panel before pushing the button for the top floor.

Nicki sighed and flipped a loose hair over her shoulder, making a ppffttt sound with her mouth as the pieces got stuck to her fingers and ended up flying back into her mouth. "Castillo was saying all these crazy words and it seemed like they'd go down better with wine."

Erik stiffened. "What crazy stuff?"

"Just family and tattoos and bros." Nicki flicked a hand and made another ppfftt sound, but this one lasted a bit longer.

"All right." Family was at the core of everything Castillo did. Erik had received that lecture many, many times, but he'd never needed alcohol after. Odd that Nicki did. "And family and bro talk needs wine, why?"

The elevator came to a stop on their floor.

Nicki lost her balance so Erik took her hand and led her down the hall to their room.

"Why did I need wine? Well, let's see, how about because I just spent the evening with a group of Mexican Mafia members after being brought here against my will. Then the head psychopath stops everything he's doing to lecture me about family and eating his cake and blah blah blah." She barked out a laugh. "If I have to do what he's doing to have family, I'm good. And like I need that princess-pink birthday party anyway. I'm *divine* on my own. I have everything I want. I don't need family."

Neither did he. But sometimes when he walked away from his sister, Rachel, his heart did this stupid thumping thing and his throat clogged a little and he had to remind himself that the only family he'd ever known was dead.

Once inside, Erik led Nicki to the bedroom with a hand on her bare back. "Did you eat something at the bar, if not then I'll order—"

"Yes, I ate at the bar." She rolled her eyes. "I'm not drunk you know, I'm just floating a little. S'all good. So, quit treating me like a child."

She had a lot more anger and awareness in her eyes than he'd believed. "Why don't you lie down then?"

"Why don't you kiss my ass?" Nicki turned on him. "So, calm, so cool, aren't you Erik? You don't drink, you don't let words reach deep inside and touch all those empty places in your soul. Nothing lights a fire in you but stupid revenge."

"You want to know what lights a fire in me?" He erased the distance between them and grinned when her eyes widened.

"I already know the answer to that. I believe I said rev—"

"No." He gripped her hair by its loose bun and tugged back her neck. "You don't know anything." And for some reason he refused to examine, he bent and kissed her. Showing her he *could* feel and he could make her feel, too. He slanted his mouth, getting a better angle as he devoured her. Her red wine flavor burned across his senses, igniting his need for a deeper taste.

She moaned against his mouth and kissed him back just as fiercely, seeking to gain power over him with her skilled tongue.

His needy cock thicker than it'd ever been made him hold her tighter, draw her closer. He drove his tongue into her mouth, tasting her, owning her, and basically losing his mind against her plump lips.

Fighting to breathe, he eased back and attacked her neck with light nips and hard kisses. Half out of his mind, he growled in her ear, "Turn around." He stripped the dress straps from her shoulders. Then kissed a path down her back before trailing back up and licking the curve of her shoulder.

She tried to turn but he held her in place, skating his fingers around her front to tug on her stiff nipples as he kissed her neck again. "*This* lights the fire, Nicki. And this is where you'll burn."

"Show me?" She drew his hand down to her panties and pressed it against her mound. She arched against his invasion and dropped her head back against his shoulder. "That's what I want."

He grinned, removed his hand, and then stepped back. "Wait. You've had too much to drink."

"Hell yes I have." Whipping around, she shoved his chest. "Why do you think I haven't punched you in the mouth for all your shit since...since, I don't know, like forever?"

"Nicki."

"Shut up, Eric. It was half a bottle...okay, and maybe a few glasses before then, too, but I'm feeling fine so don't ruin it."

"I don't even know why I asked." After watching her full breasts bounce when her arms flailed, not to mention her wild loose hair, and burnished-red lips, he didn't know why he'd resisted anyway. Done fighting, he picked her up and tossed her on the bed.

She landed with a bounce then narrowed her eyes. "Hey! Don't do that again or you'll see how much I drank."

Even with his whole world teetering on the brink, he still could laugh with this woman. But hadn't this moment been building between them for a long time? It hadn't happened because... because...no, don't think of Korzakov. Don't bring that man into this moment.

"Erik? What's wrong?" Nicki lay on the bed, naked except for her heels and black silk underwear.

Shaking his head, he unzipped his pants, tugged on his flagging erection, kicked off his shoes, and unbuttoned his shirt.

On her side, she trailed her fingers along her chest before using her index fingers and thumbs to pinch her nipples. "You better have supplies."

"I'm prepared for everything." He pulled a condom from his wallet. Then shoved off his pants and his briefs and joined her on the bed. "Are you sure you're good?"

"Yes." She cupped his cheek and arched against him.

Her wide smile and clear gaze was enough to convince him she was alert and engaged in this moment. A bit buzzed, and needing comfort...and lonely. So very lonely. Like recognized like. Plus they could both die tomorrow. Korzakov had people everywhere, so why not take this night and enjoy a beautiful woman who'd become... something to him? Was that right? He wouldn't delve into anything deeper right now.

Settling on top of her, he groaned as her smooth skin brushed against his. "It's your turn to beg."

"Do your worst."

And so he did.

He set about driving her crazy, starting with her mouth and working his way down her body, using every ounce of skill he'd ever learned.

Hot kisses, arching bodies, gasps, and moans. Wet and slick and so very ready.

She trailed her nails up and down his back before lifting her hips against his. "Take me. I'm so ready. Please. Erik."

Her uttering his name flipped a switch in his brain again. *Erik.* Yeah, that was his name. That's who he was. *Erik Pavel.*

And this woman was...she was...

She was panting and flushed beneath him. Had she looked the same when taken by his worst enemy? Had she found pleasure in Korzakov's arms?

Erik sucked in a deep breath and jerked up on his knees. Away from the heat. Away from her.

Nicki bit her bottom lip. "What is it? What's wrong?"

Jaw clenched, he stared into her hooded green eyes and released another long breath. "I'm sorry. I can't...it's just...how could you do this with him?" His stomach churned and he knew he was saying the wrong thing, but for some reason, he couldn't stop. Why couldn't he separate the two? What was wrong with him? He had no right to judge her, or anyone else for that matter.

But Korzakov's hands had touched this skin, and he'd had her body and that stopped him.

Nicki stiffened—her entire body, likely even her heart.

Then the tip of her stiletto shoved against the thin skin of his balls, maybe even piercing the flesh. Wincing, he shifted his hips but she just pressed deeper against his sensitive skin before she laughed. A harsh laugh. A fuck-you laugh filled with mockery and disdain.

Wordlessly, she shoved away and then she rose from the bed. She slid on her dress, running her fingers through her disheveled hair.

He gripped his sore balls. *What have I done?*

Head held high, she grabbed the wine bottle off the side table and walked toward the door before placing her hand on the doorframe and turning on her heel. "You know the sad truth is, Korzakov has fucked you as many times as he's fucked me. The only difference is you seem content with letting him keep his dick up your ass. And that's on you, not me. Everything I-I've done—Damn you. I won't cry over you. Screw that." Dropping her gaze, she drew a shaky breath then blew it out. "Everything I've done in my life was for survival, and I've done fine on my own. I've tried with you over and over, and we keep ending up right back here. So, stay the hell away from me, you hypocritical son of a bitch!" After throwing the bottle at his head, she stormed out the bedroom door.

Then the outer door slammed shut.

He flinched at the sound then flicked off the wine droplets that had landed on his arm as the bottle sailed through the air. "Idiot." He rubbed a hand over his stupid mouth.

The wobble in her voice.

The tears shining her eyes.

What kind of monster had he become? How could he say such a brutal thing?

He was fucked. So fucked. Because hadn't he just delivered a bullet through a woman's heart, hadn't her hair been in her eyes, and hadn't he, once again, remained frozen as everything ended?

CHAPTER THIRTEEN

Nicki kicked her shoes into the cavernous walk-in closet—the closet of a room she'd purchased with Erik's credit card. The most expensive room she could find.

She'd learned to grab and go a long time ago, and that included wallets of men who were "escorting" her. After Erik's cruel words, she'd stolen his wallet and switched to the hotel across the strip.

Alone in the bedroom equipped with shiny gold lamps, a wall-length mirror, and a black hot tub, she paced in front of the king-size bed. "Stupid judgmental jerk. He's the one who walks around with the revenge-dick stuck up his ass, and he thinks to stop mid-fuck to give me hell about who I am and who I've been with?" She clenched her hands into fists. "Oh, sorry, didn't know you were up for sainthood, jerk."

After working off her stupid black gown, balling it up, and tossing it in the corner, she rubbed her stomach when it growled. "Huh, didn't eat enough during that Mafioso bizarro birthday party, so maybe I should see if any late-night buffets are open with five hundred dollar steaks and twenty-pound lobster tails. And oh yes, more wine, of course. But only the most expensive bottles." She gripped Erik's credit card in her hand. "Take that, Pavel."

Digging into her suitcase, she found a ragged pair of jeans and a long-sleeved pink top. She slipped everything on, shoved her feet into a pair of flip-flops, and then flounced out of the room.

If Korzakov was truly out to murder her, at least she'd work in one last supper since mind-blowing sex was off the table. And it had been mind-blowing, which pissed her off even more. "Nope. Not even going to think about that jerk and his slick, hot moves. Not ever again. Because I don't need him. I'll find another man who won't throw my past in my face. Or maybe I'll find a woman who believes in helping others like I do. Who'll understand who I am now. Because I'm awesome now. I'm better. Judgmental jerks can kiss my ass. I got this."

The elevator door opened.

Still grumbling foul opinions of Erik, she stepped inside and punched the Lobby button.

The young couple already inside gave her the side-eye before shifting into the corner. Well she had been yelling at herself, pacing, and waving her arms like a crazy person.

"Sorry." She glanced at the couple. They were likely on their honeymoon and stupid in love. "Didn't mean to scare you. Just been hitting the sauce." After miming sucking down a bottle, she snickered at their expression before sailing out the elevator and winding her way through the casino.

Most of the slot machines had been updated so no actual coins fell, which seemed a travesty on a lot of levels. "What's wrong with using coins, huh?" She hollered loud enough for an old lady with an oxygen tank to stop and stare. "Apparently, coins aren't good enough for some people. Some people have to have shiny new shit and don't appreciate things for the classics they are."

The old lady shook her head and went back to her game.

Nicki couldn't blame her. She could only hope that she'd hold onto this anger for a very long time, because she refused to feel dirty or ashamed. And yet, she knew once the fury and rage subsided that's exactly how she'd feel, and she damned Erik Pavel all the more.

NICKI DROPPED her plate of perfectly pink prime rib on the table next to her monster salad. A load of crab legs teetered off the edge of the salad plate.

Before leaving her new hotel, she'd asked the concierge for the most expensive buffet within walking distance and now here she was. After she inhaled this mongo salad and her load of beef, she'd hit that dessert bar like a boss. Hot fudge was definitely in her future.

Now that the wine had somewhat left her system, she viewed her participation in tonight's events rationally. They were two people locked in a dangerous situation, which heightened all sorts of emotions, so of course the possibility of them exploding into bed existed. His words were cruel and unnecessary, and she accepted the fact that Erik Pavel was not worthy of her friendship or her concern. She would find another way to stay safe from Korzakov. And that was that. With a past as sordid as hers, she had to compartmentalize and then slam those mental doors shut. Reliving the past never helped, and never changed anything. She'd keep moving forward, because what other choice did she have? Maybe she'd move. A change of scenery would be nice, and she had too many bad memories in Ohio. With Ariel. With Erik. Perhaps, she'd go someplace warm and tropical.

She ruminated on acceptable places while people watching and digging into her salad. *I'm okay. A little stung, but overall, I'm fine.* She'd been through worse. A lot worse.

A tall, red-haired man kept glancing her way as he filled up his plate.

Great.

He approached her table, sunflower seeds spilling off his salad. "Can I join you?"

"Um, no." Because she and her prime rib were about to have a moment and she didn't need some man around to hear her moans of ecstasy.

The man plopped down anyway. He wasn't bad looking, but he was quite a bit older than her so...gross. Been there done that, buddy. Just ask Erik. He seems to know all about it. *Oh yeah, you're over it, all right.*

After shutting down her stupid mental argument, she pointed her fork at the man. "Listen guy, I just want to eat my—"

"Nicki, Nicki, Nicki." He shook his head. "You shouldn't have run off on your own."

Her stomach churned, and she eased back in her seat. Damn him for jacking up her meat-eating moment. She glanced at her steak knife before grabbing it and tapping it against the table. "First off, I won't leave this room without a fight and everyone here will catch our ruckus on their cell phones. Then a massive manhunt will ensue for a crazed brunette and a tall ginger. You're easy to pick out of a crowd, so nix that idea right now. And my second point, if you're here to kill me for Korzakov, can you just slip something into my iced tea so I can drift peacefully into death after my meat coma?"

The man stared at her for a moment then folded his arms on the table, pushing his plate forward and bumping into her plate of crab legs. If he spilled her melted butter, things would get ugly. She'd had enough of bullies tonight.

"Erik didn't want to join you for dinner after Castillo's party?"

"Are you building up to something? Because I already comprehend that you've been following me. Don't need the play-by-play of my evening, but thanks anyway." She lifted her knife and sliced into her prime rib before taking a big juicy bite. "Oh, this is heaven."

"These little moments in life are nice, aren't they? But then *we* know what it's like to be locked away like an animal, don't we?"

Oh, so the guy was going for camaraderie and he'd chosen prison. Of course that would work. Who wouldn't want to be friends with an ex-con? *Idiot.* "If you're referring to my time in prison, then yes, I will say I do have an appreciation for good food after that slop. But what are they supposed to feed us? Hell, I ate better there than when I was a kid. Anything is better than an empty stomach."

He stabbed a cherry tomato from his salad and waved it in the air with his fork. "We were both sent to prison for crimes we didn't commit."

Nicki noted the jagged scar around his neck. Creepy as hell. "Ah...I know who you are now. Aren't I a little old for you?"

He turned and gave her a look. A look that sent a chill down her spine, because this guy was capable of disgusting things. "Your attempt at humor isn't the slightest bit funny. You all laugh at something you don't understand."

"Daddies with their daughters is called incest. I understand, because I can open any dictionary in the world and it's defined right there. However, you're right, it's not something anyone should joke about." Her salad started to sour in her stomach. She could take her knife and stab him, but she'd have to be quick. Or she could dial 9-1-1, or Erik—No, she wasn't that desperate.

"We'll agree to disagree and set that topic aside for a moment."

Nicki arched a brow and flicked her fingers toward another table. "How about you do that someplace else entirely? That'd really work best for me. Thanks. I don't believe I asked for a side of pedophilia."

After narrowing his eyes, he breathed deeply through his nose. "Erik has many, many enemies."

"Right, yes." She dipped another piece of meat into the au jus before covering it in horseradish sauce. Though her stomach was unsettled, she wouldn't waste this food. "I'm one of them, but do go on with your nefarious scheme."

"I've been given a few tasks by Korzakov. One of them being to destroy Erik in all possible ways. Take down everything that means something to him. I'm all for that, and I have a plan."

"Oh, evil plans. I'm tracking with you." She nodded and wiped her mouth with a napkin.

He gripped her arm and squeezed. Hard. "Do *not* play with me, young lady. I'm doing you a favor by giving you this warning. Next time you see me, I won't be as nice and you won't be so glib."

"Let go of my arm before I scream bloody murder."

McCord grinned. A know-it-all grin. An I've-got-you-now grin.

Nicki fought back a shiver.

"As you said, everyone in this place will record what happens with their phones, but none of them will help you. I could grab that knife out of your hand and slit your throat in less than a minute and no one will stop me. I'll walk out of here with the knife in my hand and disappear. Keep pushing and see what happens."

Nicki glared at his hand *still* on her arm.

He released her. "As I was saying, I have a plan, and since you're sitting here alone, I thought I'd let you in on it. I'll finish what Korzakov has asked of me while at the same time destroying everyone keeping me from my daughter. I'll toy with Erik for a while, and then deliver him to Korzakov to do with as he pleases."

Nicki just nodded because she didn't want McCord touching her again with his disgusting hands. She thought again about stabbing him with her knife. She could end him, too. She could stop all this killing before it began. But he was tall, and thickly muscled, and probably had loads of practice after shanking a bunch of badass dudes in prison. She'd end up dead and bleeding on the floor with a steak knife in her throat.

"Nicki?" One of Castillo's men who'd been hovering around the mafia leader all night, stepped up to their table. "Everything okay here?"

Raul? Was that his name? She tried not to show relief or gratitude in her expression. "Everything is perfect. This man was just leaving."

McCord nodded. "I was." He stood and tucked his chair back into the table so hard that it toppled her tea, which spilled onto her half-eaten prime rib.

"Hey! What the hell?"

The smug bastard tugged down his shirt then gave her a two-finger salute. "Be seeing you soon, Nicki."

CHAPTER FOURTEEN

"Rachel's not supposed to even be here." After arriving home from Vegas, Erik stood toe to toe with Bronco, his sister's fiancé and jabbed a finger against the pro-football player's chest.

He'd arrived back at his apartment after letting Castillo handle Nicki's return. She was occupying one of Erik's "safe" houses, and he'd come to one of his own, only to be followed inside by his sister and her big lug boyfriend. "Rachel's supposed to be on a deserted island somewhere. Not here where Korzakov can torture then kill her, Bronco. We discussed this."

Rachel grabbed Erik's arm. "Don't you dare get angry with him. It's all over town about the feds raiding Korzakov's place and the arrest of his accountant. If you think I'm not helping you bring him down, and that I won't protect you as much as I can while I'm doing it, you're wrong."

Her voice broke at the end and her eyes glistened.

"I don't want or need your help, Rachel." He refused to let her emotions sway his own, because the threat to her was very real.

"I owe you."

"Stop. Just stop." Erik paced in front of the ratty brown couch—

the only piece of furniture in this safe house. "You don't owe me anything and you need to stop thinking that you do."

Bronco placed strong hands on Erik's shoulders and glared down at him with his light-blue eyes. The mammoth was six-six, almost three hundred pounds of solid muscle, and the left guard on the Manchester Marauders offensive-line. "You're not the only one with connections and money, Pavel. We do this as a team."

Erik barked out a laugh. If they could find him, so could everyone else. And wasn't that so kind of Rachel to make sure they were all convened in one place? Korzakov could pick them off one at a time like a shoot-the-duck game at the county fair. He rounded the couch, spread open a space in the dust-covered plastic blinds, and glanced out the window. "You need to leave, Rachel. And I need to find somewhere else to stay."

Rachel shook her head. "We have other people working behind the scenes. As Bronco said, you're not the only one with resources."

No. She couldn't help him. Korzakov was too dangerous. Erik faced his sister. "I don't want you here. Nor do I want you in my life. I thought I made that clear."

"Pavel, don't be a dick." Bronco crossed both arms over his formidable chest.

"Listen, you dumb jock, take this woman and get out of town. You may be a badass on the football field, but this is real life."

"Don't you dare call Bronco dumb." Rachel stomped over to stand in front of Erik. "You don't want us involved but we are, and you damn well better believe we're going to protect ourselves any way we can. We aren't stupid." She jabbed a finger in Erik's face. "I know you don't want me in your life. Well, too bad, because I am. The same blood runs through me as it does through you. I failed you once before, and I won't do it again. So push me away, use your cruel words against me, but don't you dare attack Bronco. *He* didn't do anything to you. As a matter of fact, he puts up with far too much from this family as it is."

Family. There was that word again. Erik ignored the ache in his heart and hardened his gaze. "Whatever precautions or plans you have won't be enough. Use your connections to hide and leave. How many times do I have to tell you this!" He considered what he could say, and how hard he could push to get Rachel out of his life forever. Maybe he'd sidestep her and go after Bronco instead. He seemed to be her Achilles heel.

"I talked to Nicki," Rachel said.

"Oh, Jesus." Of course, she'd drop that bomb. Erik huffed out a sigh before schooling his features. He'd done what he had to do in pushing Nicki away. He couldn't have planned it any better, actually. Her hating him was for the best. *If that's the case asshole, why can't you look your sister in the eye?*

"She told me *all* about your trip to Vegas. And here I didn't think you could be any bigger of a heartless jerk."

"None of that is any of your business." He put steel in his tone. Nicki was an off-limits topic for his sister—and for him.

"She's my friend. She's in danger because of a mistake I made a long time ago. And she's relying on *Frankie Castillo* to keep her alive. The entire thing makes my head explode. I hate that all these pieces are in place because I walked away from you for a moment at a park twenty years ago."

"Rachel, I swear to—"

"No. You've got far too many things going on at once. And then,"—she practically shrieked—"Ted McCord is your partner? Really? What the hell, Erik?"

"Wasn't my idea to pair with him."

"Right, then you let Sheridan beat him? What were you thinking?"

"That isn't how it happened." He rubbed his temple, fighting off a massive headache. "How do you even know what she did?"

"Because she's my partner's *pregnant* fiancée, you stupid ass!"

"Clayton's the one that can't control his woman. I didn't ask her to be there."

"We're getting off point here." Bronco placed a hand on Rachel's arm.

She glared at him before she breathed deeply and nodded. "Right. So, here's what's going to happen."

"I already said what's going to happen." Erik gritted his teeth and clenched his hands into fists at his sides. "Get the fuck out of my life. I don't want a family. I don't want a sister, and I sure as hell don't want a half-ass detective who thinks she's tough planning anything. You're right. It *is* your fault I'm like this. What kind of person leaves a three-year-old alone in a public park?"

She gasped.

But he just kept on building that wall. She had to get away from him, and if he had to be ruthless to keep her safe, he would. "Do whatever the hell you're going to do. Get your tiny ass killed and see if I give a shit. All of this could've been prevented if you'd just been—"

Bronco grabbed his shirtfront. "That's enough, Pavel."

"Fuck you."

Bronco reared back and punched him in the face.

Erik's head jerked back, but he didn't go down. Flashing a cocky grin at the big guy, he rubbed his jaw. "You think I haven't been beat down before?"

"Bronco, that's enough." Rachel wedged her way between them and placed a hand on her fiancé's arm.

"Her death..." Bronco pointed a finger in his face. "It matters. You don't get to say it doesn't. Not after everything she's done for you. You don't say that ever."

"Her death must not matter to you either or else you'd listen to what I'm saying."

"Erik, I wouldn't push him again."

"Fuck you, too, Rachel."

"That's right, push and push until you're alone again. Until all that comforts you is your revenge. That's okay. I can live with everything you've thrown at me. I deserve it. After all, you are who you are because of me."

"Rachel, God damn it." Bronco tugged on her arm.

"No." She held up a hand and faced Erik again. "Do you know how much it kills me to see you like this? To stand here as you push me away with your cruel words? To hear how you treated Nicki, and to know if I had just been more aware, I could've prevented everything?"

Though he hated that she believed such a thing, he grabbed onto her guilt and used it against her. She had to back away from him forever. He had to make her see she didn't belong in his world. "You're right about that, Rachel. You fucked up and you're fucking up again, so—"

Bronco's fist smashed into his face again.

This time Erik did go down. But if he had to make them both hate him so they'd leave, he would.

"Baby, don't say that." Bronco held Rachel's face between his hands. "Please, you gotta stop with this guilt. You've tried so hard. It's time to let the past go. Please, see that. We're doing what we can, but you have to walk away from him. He's poison."

"No, he doesn't mean it," Rachel whispered as tears fell down her cheeks. "And h-he's...he's my brother."

Bronco's jaw clenched, and he stared down at Erik. "Her love, when she gives it, is unconditional. And you don't deserve that. It tears me up inside and pisses me off, but her loyalty and tenacity is why I love her. So go ahead and wound her with your words. But someday you'll wish you'd held her tight. Someday you'll wish you'd seen what a beautiful person she can be." Bronco drew Rachel against his side. "Get your head out of your ass. You think I *want* Rachel to help you? Do you think I want her to have anything to do with you? I lie awake at night scared to death that I'll lose her. And deep down, I know you do, too. That's the only reason I'm not barreling into you like a training sled right now."

Rachel heaved a big sigh and rested her forehead against Bronco's chest. "Let's go. I can't be here anymore."

Bronco led her to the door.

Erik watched them go then stood because he didn't stay down for anyone. No one understood his decisions, but then again, they hadn't walked in his shoes. Why should he have to keep apologizing for who he was? Maybe sometimes he did wish he could see Rachel as a real sister, but how could he ask that of her, when his soul was so dirty and broken? And now her very life was in peril because of the choices he'd made. He never should've reentered her life. He'd add that decision to his long list of regrets.

Rachel stopped at the door and then turned around. "I don't expect an apology."

Erik grunted and rubbed his sore jaw. "Good, because the only words you'll get from me are, why are you still here?"

Rachel kept on as if he hadn't spoken. "But you *do* owe Nicki one. What you said to her was unforgiveable, but that doesn't mean she doesn't deserve to hear the words." She shook her head. "Instead of living your life for revenge, consider living it for redemption... starting with your own."

And with that she turned on her heel and walked out.

Heart pounding, he rushed to the window, sure his sister would be murdered on the sidewalk in a rain of bullets. But she and Bronco made it to their car and drove off.

Rachel was a complication he didn't need. Her attempts at playing some kind of super-woman didn't have him contemplating revenge or redemption. No, his new word of the day was resolve.

Resolve to take care of her once again. Because one truth was universal: family could hurt you the most.

A fact Korzakov knew all too well.

CHAPTER FIFTEEN

Raul entered the bedroom with a huge bouquet of red roses. "These came to the bar for you."

Nicki set her E-reader on the side table, slightly irritated at being interrupted during a particularly naughty sex scene. The roses' sweet floral scent hit her nose as Raul placed them on an old wood dresser.

"So cliché." She rolled her eyes. Regardless of how beautiful the flowers were, they still annoyed her. Everything annoyed her today though. Which had to do with being stuck in this house in the middle of a small town just east of Manchester, Ohio with a bunch of men she didn't know all because of Erik Pavel. Plus, who knew if she'd have her job when she got back. Missing work for days on end never went well with employers. She'd have to start over. Again. So, the flowers did not make her heart melt nor were cartoon birds and butterflies fluttering in front of her eyes. As a matter of fact, she'd prefer to toss the whole bouquet against the wall.

"You're not curious about who sent them?" Raul cocked a dark brow.

He was dressed as she was in a T-shirt and jeans. Though his skin was covered in tattoos. She should get one. Right now she'd chose a big-ass middle finger right in the middle of her forehead. "Not really. Don't care. Flowers are stupid."

He opened the card anyway. "They're from Erik. He wants to meet you for lunch."

"Oh, sure. Do you have any poison lying around so I can kill him? Preferably something that'll make his bowels explode for days before he crumbles to his death."

Grinning, Raul tapped the card against his hand. "A vicious woman. I like it."

Nicki frowned. "I'm sure you do."

He chuckled. "Erik watches you, you know."

"Well he *is* a creep."

"No, he watches you like a starving man."

"For your information, he took a big bite then spit it out." Nicki smiled sweetly then pressed her Kindle's On button, ready to escape into the story again.

"He's a fool then." Raul gave her a thorough once-over before winking.

"I agree." She tipped her chin then held out her hand. "May I see the card, please?"

He handed it over.

Nicki,

Meet me at the diner on Friday at 2pm

Erik

Nicki ripped the little card into pieces.

Raul sat down on the bed beside her. "Not interested, eh?"

"Nope."

"He's not a good man. You know this, right?"

"No...I mean, yes, right, he's not good."

"Still, I have to admire his single-mindedness. He's lived his life with one goal in mind and now he's seeing it through. He's ruthless and he's doing it all because he lost someone he loved. If he makes it through this alive, I'd think it'd be nice for a woman to be on the receiving end of that kind of loyalty."

Nicki huffed out a laugh. "Well, I won't be receiving anything. And it sounds like maybe you and Erik have something in common, because none of what he's doing makes any sense to me."

"Doesn't it?" Raul stared across the room. "Pavel abducted Erik from his biological family. Then Korzakov killed his stand-in mother. What do you expect Erik to be other than the animal they made him? They taught him to bite back and that's what he's doing."

"Maybe so, but he's hurting just as many people along the way."

"He doesn't care."

"I'm well aware." Nicki sniffed then ran a finger along the edge of her E-reader.

"That's the way it has to be for him to finish. For him to become the man he needs to be, he has to fulfill his vow."

"Revenge isn't a life plan, Raul." She stared into the man's deep brown eyes.

"Ah, but for some, it is."

"Is it for you?"

He patted her knee and stood. "Castillo is meeting with Erik on Saturday. You'll see him then."

"Oh boy, a fieldtrip." She clapped her hands together, hoping he'd catch her sarcasm.

Raul shook his head and ambled out of the room.

After watching him leave, Nicki poured the ripped card's tiny bits from one hand to the other. Raul seemed different than the rest of the men. He seemed more...refined. He rarely spoke when he was with the others, but he was always watching. She'd been around enough bad guys to know when one was good. She considered his words about Erik's motivation, but after the way Erik had treated her in Vegas, she still didn't feel anything but betrayal. And a lot of, 'who does he think he is to judge me'?

Why would Erik wish to meet with her after he'd made clear his true opinion? Nothing remained between them. Nothing.

He couldn't see her as anything but a vessel once used by his greatest enemy, and she wouldn't see herself as anything but a vessel for good and for change—for herself and for other women like her. Hopefully she'd live long enough to fulfill that goal. She'd made an appointment to meet with Andrea Martin at Turning Pages later this week. Now she'd look like a clueless fluff-head when she didn't show up. *Dang it!* She really wanted to tour the facility and see how she could help the women under Andrea's care. One more frustration to lay at Erik's door. "Nope. He is now under the heading of he-who-shall-not-be-named. Like that villain in those kid's books." She lifted a finger into the air and used her best wizard voice to declare, "He shall not pass. Wait...that's not right. I'm mixing up characters."

With a slight chuckle, she rolled out of bed. Standing beside the bouquet, she ran her fingers across the roses' silky petals. They were stuck in a vessel, too. Thorns and all.

She pulled them free and tossed them up in the air, letting them land and stay wherever they chose to fall.

CHAPTER SIXTEEN

Squinting against the glare of the summer afternoon, Korzakov strode out of the courthouse. He'd expressed his displeasure over having to come downtown. Spending the day mingling with the dregs of society was not how someone of his caliber lived. The majority of the people inside that building would do well to sign up for a lesson in hygiene. The stench of moral decay was a ripe combination of body odor and rotting teeth. He'd need to shower when he returned home.

But first he had to run the gauntlet of viperous reporters.

Heaving a sigh, he switched to his prescription sunglasses and charged down the steps.

A short blonde reporter, with entirely too much makeup, shoved a microphone in his face, blinking her dark lashes as she barked out question after question.

He considered grabbing the microphone and shoving it down her throat. Bitch would probably like it.

How dare she question him? Leeches, the lot of them.

Yegor elbowed the woman out of the way. "Sir, stay right behind me."

Korzakov shot the man a glare. Where else was he supposed to go? And why hadn't the head of his security thought to bring more backup?

Questions were shouted from all sides. Bodies pressed against him.

"Is it true your corporation helped thousands of Americans file false income tax returns?"

"What about your ties to the Justice Department and allegations of bribery?"

"Did you fund weapon sales to foreign entities?"

Gaze forward, Korzakov tugged on his tie and surged through the crowd.

"Stay back." Yegor knocked an over-aggressive cameraman to the ground.

He hadn't even been that close, but Yegor liked to push and shove, which had always been a plus in his favor.

Korzakov's lawyers had used loopholes in corporate law to dig him out of this mess, because hadn't he paid his government contacts for years to get certain laws passed. His lawyers were finally earning their outrageous monthly fees. For now. If they failed, he'd be out of this country in a heartbeat and living on his offshore funds. Not his choice, and one Erik Pavel would pay for dearly. He didn't appreciate the kid's machinations. He'd let the events unfold as they would. But now that he'd seen the entire game board, he was ready to play. And he'd win by cashing in on favors owed to him by powerful people.

He tried peering around Yegor's bulky frame. "Is Georgy bringing the car around?"

"Yes, sir. He's right up front."

Korzakov grunted when he caught a glimpse the double-parked Range Rover.

"Have you heard from that snake, Raul?" He wiped the sweat from his brow with his pocket square.

"No, sir." Yegor held open the SUV's back door, blocking the reporters with his body.

Korzakov slid into the backseat.

Yegor shut his door then settled his big frame in the front passenger seat.

"Take me to the downtown office. I need privacy." Pulling his phone from his pocket, he ignored the cameras and the plastic women asking questions through the window. Such madness. What did they think he would do? Conduct an interview behind a tinted window?

The vehicle eased away from the curb, and moved forward in short bursts.

"Just fucking run them over, Georgy. Damn idiots."

His phone rang with an unavailable number.

"Korzakov."

"It's Raul." His voice came across as if he were trying to speak without being overheard.

Jaw tight, Korzakov gritted out, "You think to call me now after you helped Erik Pavel escape the lumberyard? Not only that, you put my man in the hospital for a day."

"I have word."

"I don't need information now." He tugged his tie loose. "I needed it when these sons of bitches were interrogating my accountant and raking through my finances."

"We have a package that will be delivered on Saturday."

"What kind of package?"

"It's meant for Erik."

"Is that so."

"Yes, I thought you might want to stop the package and see her for yourself. I suggest you stop us around noon on Route one twenty-four."

Castillo's inside man had yielded nothing so far. This small offering wasn't anything he was willing to waste his time on. Plus the dirty Mexican was likely setting a trap. "I'll send Yegor to pick it up."

"No, you'll want to see this for yourself."

Korzakov tightened his grip on the phone, imagining Raul's neck under his hand. "You think to direct me?"

"Just a suggestion. *She's* a fine bit of horseflesh, sir."

The veiled message Raul was sending clicked in Korzakov's mind. "A *dark-haired* beauty?"

"The darkest."

"Green eyes?"

"The greenest."

"I see." Korzakov thumbed the location and time into his phone's Notes app. "See you then." He hung up and then flipped the phone over and over in his hand. "Yegor, have our contacts discovered any further information on Raul?"

"No."

"Interesting. He just called to inform me that he has Nicki."

"Did he say that?" Yegor glanced back, his brow furrowed.

"Of course he didn't." Korzakov rolled his eyes. "Remember our many conversations about what to say and when to say it. Ears and eyes are everywhere."

The man just grunted. "Are we picking her up?"

"Why, Yegor?" Korzakov arched a brow. "Do you want another taste of Ms. Nobles?"

The man grinned and faced forward, slapping his brother on the shoulder as they both laughed.

"So do I, Yegor." Korzakov licked his lips. "So do I."

CHAPTER SEVENTEEN

On their way into town on Saturday, Nicki chomped on her bubble gum and watched the cornfields go by while considering once again a change of scenery. As an esthetician and massage therapist, she could work anywhere, so wouldn't a new job next to the ocean be wonderful? No more of the Midwest's changing seasons. She could make new friends. Obtain new clients. Walk shoeless on a warm beach and just live without painful reminders of her past filling her life.

She would make the change. She'd done it before. She and Ariel had left behind a trailer park in Southern Virginia all those years ago. She could start over on her own this time.

Raul sat in the passenger seat of the full-size van. She was in the far back with two of Castillo's men seated in the second row of captain's chairs. A Cadillac followed with four more of Castillo's men. They were about an hour into their two-hour drive.

She'd read a little from her Kindle but now that the story was over and the couple had found their happy ever after, she'd turned to looking out the window and contemplating her future. Maybe she'd change her name to something ridiculous like in the book she'd just read. *Autumn Storm*. Who had names like that? She didn't much look like an Autumn anyway. Maybe more of a Winter. She could be Winter Snowdrop. How much would it cost to change her name anyway? She could grow organic plants and make her own cosmetics line out of lavender and seaweed. Her logo could be a big purple Loch Ness Monster or something. Seemed doable.

She blew a big bubble. It popped and left a mess of sticky pink on her lips.

Rubbing off the gum, she halted with a finger against her upper lip as two big black SUVs whipped by on the other side of the highway.

The hairs on the back of her neck rose as if on high alert. *Oh shit.* "R-Raul, did you see those two vehicles?"

He twisted in his seat but was texting, his fingers flying over the keyboard.

The two men in front of her racked their guns. Huge gold-plated guns that were completely decked out with jewels and what looked like their initials or designs or something. Was this to tell them apart? Seemed a little over the top to bedazzle a gun.

"Do you have another gun?" She cleared her throat. "Maybe something a little...ah...smaller though?"

Raul glanced back at her. "You know how to shoot?"

"Yes."

"Knowing how and being willing to kill are two different things."

"If it's them or me, I won't have a problem."

He grunted then said something in Spanish to the guy sitting to her left. The man met her gaze before pulling a plain 9mm from the bag at his feet.

Huh? No etchings or gold on this gun. She grasped the cold steel in her hand. Maybe those SUVs were not even meant for them. Perhaps they were just paranoid.

Raul started yelling into his phone, and the driver accelerated.

Nicki dared a peek out the back window and saw the two SUVs right on the Cadillac's ass.

Not good. Heart racing, she ducked in the seat, racked her gun, took a deep breath and exhaled slowly. She'd been in deadly situations before. As a child under the brutal hand of the men her mother would bring home. And as a young woman, under the hand of the men who'd bought her for the night. She'd fought and bled, but she remained alive. Her time to go was her time to go. But once again, she'd fight.

"This is stupid," she mumbled to herself before hollering up at Raul. "Pull over. We start shooting on the highway, and we might hit another car."

Raul ripped off more Spanish at the driver.

Damn it, why hadn't she taken a language in school?

Suddenly the van reared to the right, and dust whipped up around the sides, momentarily blocking her view.

Once the dust settled, Nicki caught sight of an abandoned flea market, which had a few decrepit wooden stands.

This was their standoff point. She'd die in a flea market parking lot. How very fitting for her life.

She inhaled through her nose. Could she pull the trigger? Could she kill someone? Should she aim for the head or the heart? Sure. Yes. She'd do all that while praying the guys in the SUVs were really bad shots.

She jerked to the side as the van careened into the empty lot. The seat belt pressed into her neck so she gripped it with her hand and held it away from her throat.

The Cadillac and two SUVs followed.

Her vision went woozy for a moment as she watched two men pour out of the vehicles followed by Otari Korzakov himself.

The two men held up their hands and yelled something.

The driver of the Cadillac motioned with his hands out the window.

Raul opened his door.

Oh hell, this was happening. The headline would read: *Mafia standoff leaves abandoned flea market awash in a gazillion gallons of blood.* "Raul, don't. Please, he'll kill you." Nicki wiped her sweaty palms on her jeans. "I changed my mind. Let's go. We can outrun them."

Raul winked before hopping down and walking to the back of the van.

"Cocky motherfu..." Mumbling the rest, Nicki shot out of her seat, because damn him, he needed back up. "Let me out." She growled at the guy in the seat by the side door.

He glared at her but both men got out and then waited for her exit.

Regardless of the fact that she was about to vomit and her heart seemed to want to explode, she trailed along behind them.

Korzakov turned his head as if scenting his prey and met her gaze.

Raul and the two men formed a wall in front of her.

"Ah, Nicki, so good to see you again. I was coming to get you, and yet here you are. So fortuitous."

"Get back in your car, old man," Raul shouted. "You're done."

"As you can see. I am not. Erik's so-called plans have done nothing because I saw them coming. What you hear in the news is what I've wanted you to hear. Now come with me, Nicki and we'll be on our way."

Three more men piled out of the black SUVs and stood at Korzakov's side. Did they give these psychos radioactive meat or something? Had Korzakov put a help wanted ad in the paper that said, only dudes with eighty-two inch biceps need apply? She giggled, which earned her a glare from Raul.

Shit.

And then a really stupid thought occurred. She could end this. She could shoot Korzakov right now. No one would expect it. Sure, a big shoot-out would ensue, but he'd be down. She'd practiced on the sly with a gun bought off the streets. Ex-cons weren't allowed weapons, after all.

She could do it. The only problem was her gun wasn't necessarily a kill-with-one-shot gun. Still a bullet in the right spot would knock anyone down and could kill.

Memories of the night Korzakov and the two brothers raped her scored across her mind. Then the visions switched to the little girl, barely older than ten, who'd been brought in later and tossed at Nicki's feet. Her body caked in blood, cheeks bruised, lips split open. Her eyes had been wide and vacant, likely seeing something horrific, playing on repeat in her mind. Korzakov's client had brutalized the child and then dumped her body outside one of the mafia leader's restaurants. Nicki had lain broken in her own way as Korzakov put a bullet in the girl's brain.

Ending her.

Brutally and without a second thought.

Didn't he deserve to die the same way? Hadn't he hurt enough people? She'd survived jail time once before, and she could do it again. For herself. For that little girl whose name was never known and her body likely buried in the woods never to be seen again.

The unfairness of it all knocked the breath from her lungs.

She lifted her chin. And almost as if she watched herself from above, she blocked out the stupid male bantering going on around her and crept over until she stood between Raul and Castillo's other men.

Chewing the shit out of her gum, she lifted the gun and lined the sight right between Korzakov's eyes.

Why wasn't anyone stopping her? Couldn't they see she'd lost her mind? Couldn't they hear her heart beating like mad? But there he was, the man who'd held her down, the man who'd ripped into her body, the man who would use her against Erik, and then toss her into some shallow grave.

The devil on her shoulder shouted, "Stop him! End this now!"

Cold steel pressed against her finger and then she pulled the trigger and would swear on her life forever that everything around her stopped—until Korzakov hit the ground.

Then.

Muffled shouts sounded from all around her.

Someone yanked on her arm.

Something whizzed through her hair.

Loud pops and more shouts.

Dust stirred.

She blinked, and her whole body started to shake.

Holes appeared in the side of the van.

Eyes wide, she stared at the gun in her hand.

At her side, Raul's body jerked and then he shoved her through the van's open side door.

He hustled into the passenger seat and screamed words at the driver she couldn't understand.

More pops.

And then a hand against her throat.

A fist against her face.

Pain burst upward from her cheek.

Then nothing.

CHAPTER EIGHTEEN

His entire body vibrating with rage, Erik held Nicki's hand. "Was this really necessary?"

So much to digest at once, but Nicki...her poor face. Her entire left side was an array of red and purple. They were in the guest bedroom of a local surgeon's who had an agreement with Castillo to stitch up any of his injured men. Raul was in there now getting his side cleaned up.

Castillo stood beside Erik. "That woman shot Korzakov in the head."

"I don't see why you'd mind. You wanted him dead." Erik rubbed a hand against his temple, considering all the ramifications of Nicki's actions. He had no idea where to start.

"This is true." Castillo chewed on the butt of a cigar. "But I sure as hell didn't want *her* murdering him. This is a mess."

Nicki opened her good eye and glared. "Would you shut up? My head is throbbing enough as it is without having to listen to you two."

Erik barely refrained from choking her, but her neck already had a bruise in the shape of a hand from one of Castillo's men. "Oh, you will listen. What were you thinking?"

Nicki blinked then released a long breath. "I was thinking everything would be easier if he was gone."

"Is that so? You do realize he has others working for him. Others willing to step in and take his place and their first order of business will be to slit your throat as a show of strength."

"By then I'll be long gone."

"You'll be gone all right." Erik had about lost his mind when Castillo had called to tell him Nicki had shot Korzakov. Reports from the hospital had the man in critical condition. Law enforcement had arrived at both the hospital and roadside scene, searching for information.

Castillo had assured Erik that the rural road had been deserted when his men left. Not that any of that information mattered, because now Korzakov had a means to destroy Nicki. He'd implicate her in the shooting and have her murdered in prison.

"He's right, *chica*. What you did was stupid, dangerous, and actually kind of brave. I'd commend you if I didn't want to kill you right now." Castillo clapped a hand on Erik's shoulder. "But, do not worry. I have a plan. This will actually work out well for me."

Erik narrowed his eyes. No one was killing Nicki except him. Damn it!

"How will it work out well?" Nicki croaked out the words. "I shot Otari Korzakov."

"Because I say it will be so."

Nicki just sighed and averted her gaze. "How's Raul?"

"He's fine."

Erik felt a stab of jealousy over her concern, but then quickly pushed it aside. He'd have to work with the Saudis now. He'd put off their meeting until after the Vegas trip. But to save Nicki's future, he'd align himself with the devil. The narcissistic, misogynistic, and merciless prince wasn't far off. He'd annihilate everyone. But none of that would matter to Erik, because once he shook Khaled's hand, he'd no longer be alive, because either the man would kill him or leave him without a soul. "What do you plan to do, Castillo?"

"I'll have a woman who looks like Nicki confess to the crime. I'll have my brother pull some homeless woman from Guerrero. Everyone wants to escape that place, believe me."

Nicki gasped. "You won't blame this on someone else."

Erik frowned. "Nicki, your ability to make decisions is obviously skewed."

"I won't have another take the fall for my actions."

"She will have a better life in prison," Castillo yanked the cigar bud from his lips, tossed it onto the floor, and then crushed it under his boot. "The deed is done."

Eyes wide, Nicki shot up in the bed. "Then undo it!"

Erik pressed her back. "Settle down. He's done you a favor, and you will say thank you."

She mumbled something that sounded a lot like, "the hell I will."

"Nicki," Erik growled. "You *will* thank this man."

Nicki lifted her chin and met his gaze. "I'm sorry, but I cannot. I know what this is really about, Pavel. Don't think I don't." Nicki shoved off the bed then winced and touched her cheek. "Ow!"

"What are you talking about?"

"Revenge. The only thing you *ever* talk about. And now, I've taken that from you, so you're coming in here yelling because someone got to shoot Korzakov before you. Then you're expecting me to bow down in gratitude because some other woman is taking my place in prison. I don't think so!"

"Do you want to go back to prison? Do you want to die? Because that's what happens the minute you're behind those bars."

Nicki plopped back on the bed and covered her eyes with her forearm.

After a moment, her voice drifted across the room, soft and shaky. "I wanted him dead, too. You ever think of that? He raped me. He murdered a child in front of me." She balled up onto her side. "Now it's done, and I can't take it back. I won't take it back."

Erik swallowed the lump in his throat. "All right." He went to her side and brushed his fingers through her silky hair. "It's going to be all right now."

"No, it isn't." She answered in a tiny voice.

"It is. I promise." Erik bent and kissed her cheek. "Korzakov is in a coma right now. You didn't hit him between the eyes. You hit him right above his left eye."

"Sight must've been off."

"Shut up and get some rest." Erik gripped her face in his hands and then he kissed her, plunging his tongue into her warm mouth. How dare she sacrifice herself. Her vibrancy. Her spirit. Once he had to breathe or die, he eased back and studied her wet lips, surprised she'd kissed him back.

Castillo cleared his throat then nudged Erik's shoulder. "I will speak to Khaled. This happened under my watch and I will fix it."

"No, Frankie, you can't—"

Castillo lifted his hand. "Already done. I met with him yesterday. You were taking too long."

Erik spun around. "Are you kidding me?"

"No."

"Do you know who that man is?"

"The thing about staying at the top is that the level keeps rising, and it's either sink or swim. I won't sink."

Erik widened his stance, anger rising. "You dare to take that deal from me?"

"You shouldn't have brought me into your business if you didn't want me to be a part of it."

"That's exactly right. A *part*, not all." How had he lost control so fast? First Nicki shooting Korzakov, now Castillo dealing with Khaled. Where did he fall in the scheme of things?

Castillo rubbed a hand over the tattoos on his arm. "You weren't meant for this life."

"You don't know shit about me."

Castillo glanced at Nicki and smirked. "I know more than you think." He turned for the bedroom door then stopped. "Go on with your lives and don't look back. No one will know Nicki pulled the trigger today."

With those words, he strode into the hallway, waved his men over, and they all thundered down the stairs.

Erik glared at the door. He'd be damned if he was left out of the planning at this stage. He took a step toward the door.

"Well, I don't know about you, but I'm fine walking away from this nightmare."

Erik glanced over his shoulder at Nicki. At the source of all this chaos. "How can you sit there so calmly after just shooting a man? You've completely fucked yourself."

Nicki sniffed and studied her nails. "I'll do what I've always done. Survive."

"After today, your survival isn't that simple. Korzakov will hound you forever. Castillo having another woman admit to your crime means nothing to him."

"He's in a hospital bed right now, so I have time to get away...and so do you." Nicki tilted her head. "I know you feel as if I've taken away your power...and your purpose." She rose from the bed and came to his side. "But, Erik, you've done enough. Over and over, your sister, your friends, everyone has told you to walk away. So why can't you?"

"And do what?" He forced out a laugh. "I don't know anything else."

"You could live." She gave his arm a little shake.

"I don't even know what that means."

"So figure it out."

This end to Korzakov wasn't supposed to be so easy. And wasn't supposed to be completed by someone else. After everything he'd done. All the bodies he'd buried. He didn't deserve to live. He shook Nicki off. "This isn't over."

"Wow." She barked out a laugh. "You're really in denial."

"It ends when he's dead." He fisted his hands at his sides over-come by the thought that everything was crashing around him, but nothing hurt. Shouldn't he hurt?

"Erik." Nicki approached him again, placing her hand against his cheek. "This journey you've been on ends when you accept that the entire focus of your life has changed. It ends when you realize nothing will bring your mom back and revenge was never the answer."

He shook his head, yet secretly hoped she never moved her hand and that they could remain grounded in this moment. But Nicki was...she was a light...something far brighter than he deserved. He was a cruel bastard, and he'd only hurt her again, even if in this moment, he wished that wasn't the case. "Why do you even care? After every cruel word I've spoken to you...why?"

He met her gaze but she blinked those green eyes and turned away.

"I know why you said what you did." She sank onto the bed, twisting her hands together in her lap. "If you would apologize, I'd accept it and be happy to move on from here."

Erik pressed his lips together and considered...everything. "I'm sorry, Nicki. I was cruel, but I have this constant battle waging in my head. I see only one thing, and I hate it sometimes. I do." He gripped a lock of his hair and tugged until it stung. "I don't know how to be a good man. The right man. Your man. I want so much more for you. You're so vibrant. Alive. Beautiful both inside and out, and I'm nothing but a disgusting mass of hate and lies and death. I've never deserved your friendship or your belief in me. That's why I push you away. I can see it in your eyes sometimes. This hope. Rachel has it too, but I need you both to stop." He scratched the back of his neck. "My detachment has never been about you. It's *my* total and complete self-loathing, because I cannot change. I don't even know how to try."

Nicki ran her tongue along her bottom lip before chewing on it for a moment. "Really? You're ending that speech with the whole, 'it's not you, it's me'? Was going rather well up until then. I actually shed a tear."

He threw up his hands. "What do you want from me, Nicki?"

"I don't know, Erik. I just shot a man today. I'm a little distracted at the moment, so I don't know how to handle the epiphany you're having. Ask me tomorrow...if we're both still alive."

He knelt at her feet. "I am sorry...for everything."

"And I'm sorry you think you need to push so hard. I'll get the picture soon enough and my little crush on you will be nothing but a memory."

"You have a crush on me?"

Nicki heaved a sigh. "I really don't want to talk about this right now. We need a game plan, Erik. Stick with what you know and figure us a way out of here."

He studied her for a moment. Was moving on that easy for her? He'd just poured out his heart and she didn't want to hear it? He'd never understand women. Ever. But she was right, they did need a plan, because Korzakov wasn't dead. Castillo's plans might fall through, and they couldn't stay in this safe house forever.

THE PUNGENT SCENT of coffee filtered through Nicki's nose, and she blinked awake at the dark brew's call. Yesterday afternoon, before Erik had moved her to one of his super-secret lairs, she'd taken some heavy-duty painkillers, given to her by Castillo's doctor. Once arriving at this apartment, she'd headed for the bedroom. Based on the bright light streaming from behind the blinds, she'd been out all night and into the next day. The painkillers had likely been the reason she hadn't had any nightmares, but she didn't hold out much faith that streak would continue.

Brushing her hair out of her eyes, she rolled from the lumpy bed and followed her nose to the tiny kitchen.

Light blue wallpaper hung loose off the walls, and the fridge hummed and popped as if announcing its impending death. This run-down apartment was the last place anyone would ever expect to see the fastidious Erik Pavel.

"Good morning, Nicki."

"Pavel."

Erik chuckled and waved his steaming coffee cup in her direction. "I deserve that I guess." He shook his head. "I had water and coffee, but no sugar or creamer or anything else, so I hope you like it black."

She gently fingered the side of her face. No, she didn't like coffee black, but she needed caffeine in a very bad way. She'd been banged up before—beaten, bruised—so this facial injury would sting for a while but it'd fade just like the rest.

"Grab a cup and come sit for a minute." He offered her an empty black mug, a chip along the handle.

She arched a brow. Did she really care to hear anything he had to say especially before the caffeine had time to soak into her blood stream? Hadn't he said it all last night? "I'd really like to go home. Take a shower. Move on with my life."

"Yeah, and what do you plan to do?"

Oh, so they were having a normal conversation? Well then, she would pull up a rickety chair and sip her coffee. She filled the cup and sat beside him at the tiny round table. "What do I plan to do?" She ran her finger along the cup's rim. "I guess I need to know if I can first?"

His jaw ticked. "You can."

"And you?" She met his bloodshot brown eyes, and let her heart hope just a little that he would begin to change. To maybe see her differently. *Yeah, go with that, Nobles. Might as well drop kick your heart while you're at it.*

"I need to make sure everything's...solid first."

She nodded and took a tentative sip of her coffee. It'd likely burn her tongue, but after yesterday, she was still chilled to the bone. "And then what will you do?"

"I asked you first." He grinned.

When he smiled like a schoolboy sneaking a glance at his class-room crush it tugged at her heartstrings even after everything that had passed between them. "You've always been a four-year old, you know this right?"

He shrugged and sipped his coffee. He must have stored clothes here, because he wore black sweats and a faded hunter green Marauders T-shirt. No socks. His hair was wet, which was a good thing because that meant a shower with toiletries.

"I think I'll shower." She grabbed her coffee and started to stand. Hanging with Erik Pavel when he was in this weird mood gave her the willies.

"Sit down."

Frowning, she flicked a hand in the air. "I don't know what there is left to say between us, Erik, and this mood you're in is honestly freaking me out. Mean Erik, I understand. Him and I are old pals, but this sit down and have coffee Erik, is weird, and is making my stomach all gooey."

"You say the craziest shit." He shifted forward in his chair and took her hands. "I was wrong about everything."

"Yes." She raised an eyebrow, because what the hell was this? And why was her heart practically melting all over the table? "Um, I mean...what were you wrong about?"

"I want to try again." Erik pressed his warm lips against her hand.

"Try what?"

"You."

"Me?" Maybe more caffeine would clear her mind, because he couldn't be saying what she thought he was saying, could he? But if she reached for her drink, she'd have to let go of his hand, and the feeling was kind of...nice. Still, this *was* Erik Pavel, and he was a jerk. "Try me as what? Some sort of pity thing? And *again* would imply there was a before and there was no before so...I'm confused."

"I want to show you...and myself I can be something else. That past demons won't affect...well...my future."

"I can't be some sort of clean slate for you." Oh, hell. Erik Pavel had just used the word future. Maybe she'd taken one too many pain pills last night and she was still dreaming.

"I need you to try." He squeezed her hand and looked at her with something a lot like hope shining in his brown eyes.

She gasped. "Who the hell are you right now? And not only that, I kind of stopped caring what you needed when you kicked me out of your bed."

"I won't this time." He ran a finger up her arm.

Nicki scoffed and slapped at his hand. "I've been told my pussy is magical, but it isn't a cure for whatever is wrong with you, Pavel."

"I don't want a cure so much as I want to be close to someone."

"Are you for real right now?"

"Probably not." He shook his head.

"How about I just give you a hug?"

"I want you Nicki. Let me make you feel good. I need to apologize."

"Weren't you the one who said not to use sex as a replacement for something else?"

"I also *just* said I was wrong about everything. Sex *is* a replacement for a lot of...feelings. I have this intensity of something, right here"—he pressed a hand against his breastbone—"for you. And I don't know what to do with it other than to give it back to you in some way. Sex is the only way I know how, because we both know, I'm horrible with words."

"That the truth," Nicki mumbled.

He grinned. "Let me express what you mean to me. Just once."

She squeezed her thighs together because his tone and those hope-filled eyes were doing things to her innards. Naughty things. "Uh...saying sorry works just fine."

He brushed a hand down her chest and across her hard, traitorous nipple.

"Let me have you once. Let's douse this fire between us...just once. And at the end you'll go your way and I'll go mine."

"God, I really hate your face right now. If we do this thing, it'll be just once. I'm leaving. Pulling up stakes. Moving on. Because damn it...yesterday sucked...I was scared to death. I had to shoot a man. Bullets were flying. Castillo's men tried to choke me on the floor of a nasty ass van. I almost died. Do you realize that?"

"Yes, and I'm sorry for it."

"Stop saying sorry. It's annoying."

He nodded and held out his hand. "Once?"

She placed her hand in his and squeezed. Like a lifeline. Like he could actually bring about a sense of calm. Like she wasn't really saying goodbye.

But she was.

CHAPTER NINETEEN

Following him into the bedroom, she tried to separate her heart from her mind.

This was about comfort and release, nothing more.

It was one person offering solace and seeking to make amends.

That was all.

She'd let each motion play out like scenes in a movie.

Beside the bed, Erik lifted off her shirt then removed his own.

He undid her bra then tugged down her jeans.

He pulled down his own pants, no underwear beneath.

Her breathing went ragged, and all she could smell was lavender and cedar.

His cock stood at attention at his waist, the head swollen and the veins bulging along the tight skin.

Something feral fought to rise within her. She wanted to take. To rip and tear, and bear his heart, so she could own it. A voice screamed from deep in her soul to abandon the script and fly free, but that path only led to her picking up the pieces of her shattered heart.

So, she stood still as he removed her panties.

He clambered up onto the bed. "Come here." He held out his hand.

An offering. A promise of more.

Tears threatened, but she didn't know why. They weren't part of this script, and she refused to make this moment any more real than it had to be.

Following him onto the queen-sized bed, she bent over him and locked her hand around his neck before drawing him close for a kiss. A soft kiss, exploring, deep, but not urgent or harsh. Not anything but a step to the next level. Tongues delving, lips meshing—the kiss went on and on as if they both knew once they stopped, they'd be closer to the end. And maybe that's why her throat felt so clogged and her heart beat too fast, because the end *was* coming.

But just once before she walked away and started over by the sea.

With each kiss, the waves of desire rose higher and higher. His soft touches. The light flavor of coffee on his tongue. The way his muscled chest moved with each breath.

Her body seemed to float, yet waited anxiously for the next wave to crash against her skin.

And the play went on.

He kissed her neck.

Then down her chest.

She arched and sighed as he brushed his flat tongue across her nipples.

Never had she ever felt so much, so fast, and hadn't she known it would be this way? Weren't they connected on so many levels? Didn't they understand each other as no one else ever would? If they dared, couldn't they be more?

But no.

Just once.

Her hips lifted as another wave crested.

His tongue pierced her core, sending exquisite pleasure through her body.

Why couldn't this last? This feeling of being exactly where she belonged. Was this what she'd fought her whole life to find? Pleasure without pain and a lightness to her heart? Could she feel the same with another man? Did she want to?

She tugged on Erik's hair and brought him up for another kiss. Not gentle. Not soft. But with a message. One that said, this is glorious. This is divine. This is how two people should be.

Fighting for air, she pulled away and met his gaze. "I forgive you...for everything. I don't want anything between us anymore, and though I told you last night, know that I also mean it today."

He nodded and brushed her hair behind her ear. "Thank you for that."

"You needed to hear it, and I needed to say it."

He buried his face in her neck. "Nicki, I..."

"Just once, Erik. Please...just love me once."

He rose above her. "I think I could, you know. Out of anyone, it'd be you, but you deserve more."

"I deserve a lot of things, but that conversation can't happen between us. You can't have once and say that at that same time, so...don't."

He opened his mouth, but then closed it. After nodding his understanding, he bent to kiss and lick his way down her chest.

The slow smolder began again.

His fingers brushed against her core at just the right time and just the right way.

While settled on his side, he kissed her and teased her clit with soft flicks of his skilled fingers.

She grasped his thick cock, thumbing the leaking tip.

His lower body jerked and he groaned into her mouth.

So many words wanted to spill forth, but she couldn't say them for fear she'd reveal too much. And what was left to say? They only had this moment...but she didn't want it to end.

He rose from the bed and went to the bathroom, only to return quickly and fit his hard length with a condom.

He settled above her, kissing her long and deep before he nudged at her entrance then speared her with one hard plunge.

A wave rose. It undulated and churned.

He rocked his hips against her, his cock hitting the exact place she needed. Using two fingers, he pressed against her slick folds, finding that perfect spot to bring her to pleasure.

The waves crashed inside her.

She moaned and gripped his hips.

Still no words. And even if she had them, none could describe how she felt in this moment. Sex had never been like this with another. Everything stripped away. No barriers. So very real and raw.

An unnamed emotion drifted along her heart before catching and gripping so very tight.

Before she could decipher what that meant, he kissed her, messy and wet. His tongue mirroring the action of his dick, deep inside her body.

Everything coalesced.

His fingers pressed against her clit.

She cursed and bit her bottom lip as bliss struck in wave after wave of absolute pleasure. Intense, and yet, so right. As she reached that perfect moment, she felt a sense of drifting to some magical shore. As if she'd landed in some secret place where she finally felt as if she'd found a home after being at sea for far too long.

But that wasn't the end to this story.

Erik shuddered and shouted her name, riding out his own climax.

And wasn't he glorious in the moment.

Wasn't he so very beautiful with his neck corded and his body sheened with sweat?

She allowed a soft smile to curl her lips as his whole body relaxed and dropped upon hers.

The warmth and the weight so very welcome and everything she'd ever wanted.

Her heart thumped like mad, feeling something a whole lot like...love.

Holy shit. No, no, no.

Erik kissed her shoulder, rolled to his side, and then wrapped her in his arms.

Swallowing hard, Nicki mentally repeated two words, forcing herself to remember that this moment would only happen—just once.

CHAPTER TWENTY

Nicki waited until Erik's breathing turned heavy before slipping from the bed. Something she'd done far too many times to count, but this time the act felt very wrong. A string seemed attached to him now and it kept trying to reel her back in as she dressed and headed for the door. She should probably stay and help him figure out what to do next. Hell, even figure out what she should do, because honestly, she didn't really feel safe. Didn't trust Castillo or his agreements or whatever was happening in that situation. Either way, she had her own plan and she'd see it through. Time to move on even though a single tear slipped down her cheek when she'd taken one last look at the dark-haired man lying on the bed.

Once outside, she squinted as the sun blasted her in the face. Oh sure, sunshine and warmth when her entire body felt chilled, empty and...well, maybe a bit blue, as if she'd lost something precious.

Damn it, Nicki Nobles. Get your mind straight.

She stopped on the sidewalk for a second and considered going back. They *would* make a good team. Should she stay and fight? The l-word *had* crossed her mind, after all. Maybe they *could* start over someplace together, because she couldn't live in Ohio anymore.

No. *Don't do this, Nicki.* Don't confuse one amazing, heart-bursting sexual experience for something else. Erik had apologized and now they'd both move on.

She dug her phone from her back pocket and pulled up the Uber app. A plan formed in her mind: go home, pack, get her supplies from the salon, and hit the airport for her new place on the beach. Florida sounded good, hell, maybe she'd just drive there.

A sharp sting hit her left shoulder. "Ow."

Was that a mega-wasp? What the heck?

She glanced at her shoulder and saw a huge red dart sticking out. "Oh hell." Blinking, she tried to pull it free while simultaneously stumbling back toward Erik's place.

Her vision blurred.

She blinked and took two more steps.

Which building was his?

She tried running her finger along her phone screen to dial for help, but her fingers were all numb and acting stupidly independent of her wishes.

Swaying forward, she bumped against a huge pot of flowers placed on the side of the road. Dead. So dead. Should've stayed in bed. A giggle escaped. "I just ryhmeded...rhemded."

Thick arms went around her body. "Nicki, so good to see you." Her death dealer lifted and carried her.

"N-no." Blinking, she shoved and beat against his chest. "Who?" Shaking her head, she glanced up and into the eyes of Ted McCord. And then her head lolled back against his shoulder and her world went black.

———

NICKI BLINKED AWAKE SLOWLY and heard a low moan. Another one sounded right beside her and she jerked, but then realized they both came from her.

Her head ached. Her body ached. And her shoulder burned.

Whatever that jerk had used to knock her out had really packed a punch. Opening her eyes was not a good idea as McCord probably had more items he'd purchased from Torture-R-Us or she was being held in some kind of *Silence of the Lambs* hole. How had Buffalo Bill gotten those girls down in that hole anyway? Seemed he'd need a heavy-duty stirrup of some sort, and—Jesus, what the hell was she thinking about?

A whimper echoed in the room that most definitely hadn't come from her.

Taking a chance, she opened her eyes and saw the concrete block walls. Check. Moldy, stale basement smell. Check. Chilled air. Check. Luckily no industrial size bottles of lotion were around or a little white dog that barked incessantly. Nope. No fluffy dog. No hoses. No Buffalo Bill, prancing around in a skin-suit.

But even worse. Even sicker.

Two little redheaded girls sat directly across from her, both had their hands and feet tied.

A chill shot down Nicki's spine.

A cricket chirped from somewhere nearby.

A cobweb's strand fluttered back and forth, hanging from the single light bulb illuminating the room.

Nicki gagged because oh, this was truly hell. Sisters, most likely—one around nine, and the other a little younger. Their eyes would never glow with innocence again. They'd cower and have nightmares for the rest of their lives. She should know. And that thought above all pissed her off. Her life no longer mattered. She'd do everything she could to keep these girls safe. Likely not much given her current state of being tied just as they were, but something. She had to try something.

Someone whistling what sounded like Guns N' Roses "Sweet Child O' Mine," sounded in another room, causing the girls to stiffen. Just one more thing that would forever be in their nightmares.

A whistle signified nonchalance, as if the sick fuck hadn't a care in the world.

Nicki gritted her teeth against the aches in her body and faced the girls. "Hey, look at me."

One of the girls met her gaze, but the other simply shook her head, absolute terror clear in her eyes.

"How long have you been here?"

"I-I don't know." The older girl answered, her voice just above a whisper.

"Listen to me. You have to understand that a lot of people are looking for you."

She shook her head. "Nah, our momma don't care."

Nicki took a closer look. Cheap white tennis shoes. The younger girl with clothes maybe one size too big, generic graphic T-shirts. She recognized dollar store clothes when she saw them. And if the kid didn't think her momma would care, well, she recognized that too.

"People are looking for us. Smart people." Nicki glanced at the smaller one, who'd started to shake like crazy. "Are you sisters?"

"Yes."

"Okay."

The little girl sniffed then said, "He likes to play with my hair."

Nicki's stomach roiled, and she clamped down the nausea. "Well...ah...you have very pretty hair."

"That she does." McCord stood in the doorway. A pair of scissors in his hand.

The girls shrieked then fell against each other.

"McCord, I think—"

"No." He stalked forward, holding up a hand. "This isn't the part where you try to convince me with some backwards psychology about how you're my friend, and what I'm doing is wrong, and I don't want to go back to prison. No, Nicki, that isn't what's happening here."

"All right." Nicki nodded. She *had* considered all those things, but maybe she could keep him talking and keep his attention on her. "What's this about then?"

"I explained my plan in Vegas. I warned you, remember?"

She kept her tone calm, placating even. "Yes, I do."

He roared forward and slapped her. "I said don't. Don't pretend. It won't work." He gripped her chin in his hand.

Nicki ground her teeth together. "Listen, we can roleplay, I've done it before. I'll...I'll wear a red wig and call you Daddy. What the hell ever you need, just leave these kids alone."

He shook his head, an evil grin lighting his face and nothing but emptiness existing in his eyes. "But you don't have smooth untouched skin. You don't have tiny hands. You don't—"

"Enough, that's enough! Shut your mouth." If he got angry and killed her, he'd have to dispose of her body, right? Then maybe he'd get caught, right? *Oh hell.* "You are one sick mother fucker, and I've dealt with some really disgusting people. You don't get to sit here and list all this sick shit that gets you off. Fuck you."

And that got her a fist to the face.

She shook it off and spit blood on the floor. "Already been there and done that. Go ahead and finish me, because it takes a lot to—"

"Stop it. Just stop it." The older sister piped up. "Leave her alone."

Oh, God no. Nicki swallowed hard.

McCord turned to the girl.

Icy fear tore down Nicki's spine, but the taste of blood in her mouth made her strong and kept her from backing down. "I will get you Jenny. That's what you want, right? I'll get your daughter and give her to you."

He whipped around and sneered. "Oh, I *know* you will." Then he dropped to his knees and pulled the little girl's head into his lap.

Nicki bit her lip to keep from screaming. *Show no weakness.* "She doesn't owe you anything. She isn't Jenny. Don't use her as a substitute. Use me instead."

"I can have other girls. Jenny won't mind. She'll come to understand." McCord ran his fingers through the little girl's hair and then lifted the scissors.

Nicki's gaze remained riveted on the scissors as he lowered them into the girl's hair.

He lifted a strand and cut it. "So pretty." He held the strand in the light for a moment, seemingly mesmerized before he frowned. "No, no, wrong color. Wrong color." He jerked the girl's head up and started chopping.

Nicki screamed and yelled, basically losing her mind. No, not again. She couldn't watch another little girl die. She promised things, prayed to a higher power, and begged and begged McCord to stop. She'd give up everything, if he'd just stop.

And eventually he did.

Standing, he took the remnants of the little girl's hair in his hand and whistled once more as he left the room.

Leaving the girl on the floor where he'd left her. Her head a mess. Her soul destroyed. Her eyes wide open. Whimpers escaping from her throat.

Nicki couldn't even look at the sister since she hadn't helped the situation. She'd only added to the cacophony of terror and just madness. So much madness.

After blowing out a long breath, she closed her eyes as the tears poured down her cheeks. Her throat was raw. Snot dripped onto her upper lip. Her whole body shook with rage.

He'd broken her.

She'd become too soft and complacent over the past couple years. She knew better. Monsters were everywhere. She opened her eyes again and sniffed. Enough with the tears and the agony. She had to be stronger—for herself and these two little girls, because in all likelihood they'd die here. She'd lied earlier. No one cared enough to search them out. And that truth hurt more than any blow she'd ever received. Out of everything in her life, that one truth seemed to always remain constant.

She breathed deep and accepted her fate. Death by sicko pedophile slash incestuous pervert. And wasn't that the perfect title for the next feature on the Investigation Discovery channel?

CHAPTER TWENTY-ONE

Erik winced when he nicked his neck and blood trickled onto the razor. After swishing the razor in the water, he closed his eyes and leaned against the bathroom sink. He'd woken up alone. Of course Nicki would leave. Why would she ever stay?

Sighing, he opened his eyes and tapped his razor against the side of the sink. He'd do well to remember that Nicki Nobles deserved better than him. He'd almost gotten her murdered, along with the fact she'd shot a man and could likely still end up in jail for attempted murder. That notion worried him regardless of Castillo's plans.

He had to make sure. Had to keep his toe in the business no matter what, because Nicki's life was at stake, and he couldn't have that on his conscience—such as it was. He wasn't the type of man to sit on the sidelines. Hadn't he set Korzakov's downfall in place, and now Castillo thought to bump him out?

He'd never considered that he'd be alive once Korzakov fell. What would he do with his life now? For the safety of everyone, he should disappear for a while. Maybe come back in five years. Check in on Rachel. But waiting five years to see Nicki? Could he do that?

"She left you and it needs to stay that way." Heart heavy, he stared into the mirror and tried to see someone other than the man Pavel and Korzakov had crafted. "Who are you now?"

He could easily go legit. He'd been leading his business endeavors in that direction since Pavel had died. White-collar crime had mostly become legal anyway with all the new legislation that kept the rich in Armani suits, Aston Martin's, and French champagne. All he had to do was keep up with the laws—and Bingo!—he was set.

So he'd drift along and keep an eye on Nicki from afar.

He wiped the remaining shaving cream from his face with a hand towel. His whole revenge scheme hadn't ended this ache in his chest when he thought of his mother. He still felt empty, angry, and full of hate. Nothing had changed on the inside, just the external circumstances. If Korzakov should die, would that erase all this darkness? Would he feel as if a weight had been lifted? Likely not. The only time he felt even moderately human was when he sparred with Nicki. Or made love to her. Last night, he'd been fully present while diving into an all-encompassing pleasure more intense than any he'd ever known. But, he couldn't expect the same from her.

He'd do his best to leave behind thoughts of Nicki—and their one perfect moment.

Once again, he stared into his own eyes. "She forgave you once. Don't be a fool and think she'll do it again. Let her go." Yet the words that came from his mouth didn't align with those seeking to escape from someplace deep in his heart. A place he'd shut off or maybe had never turned on. In childhood, he was taught to be heartless and shown that if you had feelings for someone, they'd be torn from you in the deadliest way. So why, for the first time, did he wish he could learn something else?

AFTER YANKING ON HIS JEANS, Erik considered what he

should take from this place before he pulled up stakes and moved on to his next hideout.

His phone buzzed with Rachel's ringtone and for a moment he considered not answering, but something wouldn't let him. "Are you still in town?" he growled across the line.

"Well, a cheery good afternoon to you, too."

"Unless you've called to say you're in hiding, I'm busy."

"Are you? Would it have something to do with a certain person who is—"

Too many people could be listening so he cut her off. "What do you want?"

"Fine. I'm here at The Beauty Bar and Spa and there's no spa?"

"What?" He frowned and was very quickly reminded why older sisters were a pain in the ass. "I have no idea what you're talking about."

"No Nicki, no spa. I had a brow appointment this morning, and she's not here. Apparently she hasn't been here for a few days, and her boss gave me a look that suggested she wouldn't be here at all if that continued. If you're holding her as your sex slave, you need to release her so she isn't unemployed for the rest of her life."

Erik ran a hand through his hair, because drama of the female variety wasn't on his to-do list today. "Did you call her?"

"Yes." Her tone implied the, "duh."

"Did you text her?" He checked the bedroom floor for his shirt, found it, and then tugged it on.

"Again, yes."

"She's been busy these past couple days, and I don't know that she was planning on returning to that salon anyway."

"All her stuff is here. Erik, so what aren't you telling me?"

"Rachel, I don't know where Nicki is." And as he said the words, he felt a trickle of fear slide down his spine. Castillo likely hadn't had time to finalize all his pieces of the game, and Nicki *was* still in danger. Damn her independent hide for leaving without telling him. "Tell you what, go by her place and see if she's there."

"You've got a tone."

"I don't."

"You do."

"And what tone is that?" Exasperation was too small a word for his opinion of this conversation. Plus, they were wasting time.

"You're worried about her. What did you do?"

Well he *had* done her, quite well in fact. His dick rose in agreement. "Uh...what?"

Rachel sighed. "Is Nicki in trouble?"

Regardless of his recent pep talk about leaving her alone, if Nicki was in trouble, he could use a little help. Rachel was actually good at her job. Not that he'd ever tell her. "She might be, yeah. You go to her apartment, and I'll talk to my...people."

"Erik...are you okay?"

"Yes, why wouldn't I be?"

"Because if something happens to Nicki..."

His stomach sank, and he swallowed hard.

"She matters to you."

"It can't matter that she matters."

"You are so stupid. Go do your thing, and I'll do mine and maybe someday you'll see."

"See what?"

"That people love you. I love you. And I'm pretty sure Nicki does, too. You better find her, so I can see you happy and finally go on with my life without all this crushing guilt."

"Rachel." He couldn't have this conversation right now.

"Pffftttt. Go find your girl."

ERIK BURST out onto the sidewalk, sporting a gray hoodie in spite of the warm, sunny day, but he needed a disguise if he planned to be out in the open. He blinked against the bright rays and headed for his car parked along the street.

He'd tried texting and calling Nicki and had received no response. He'd ignored his sister's words, because the whole love thing wasn't real. Rachel might love a representation of what a brother was supposed to be, but she didn't love him. And Nicki...well, that thought didn't bear contemplating. Not when she could be dead even now because of him.

He thought of her soft sighs and her soft lips. During their moment together, he'd experienced a completeness and pleasure so different and so much stronger than anything he'd ever felt before. What had it all meant? And why with her? Cursing the green-eyed beauty for making him feel and likely being in some sort of danger, he zipped over to Castillo's as if the hounds of hell were riding his ass, because they were. Nicki needed him, and his own issues, dangers, and thirst for vengeance would have to take a back seat for now.

At a stoplight, he pressed Rachel's number on his cell.

Her voice came through the car's speakers. "Erik."

"Anything?"

"She's not here."

"Are you alone?"

"No, Bronco's here."

"Good."

"What now?"

"I need some time. Just wait at her place and see if she shows up. She mentioned something about leaving town, but I wouldn't think she'd leave without packing first."

"Nothing's packed up here. And did you say she's leaving town?"

"Yes."

"Oh, Erik."

He couldn't deal with Rachel's sympathetic tone. "Just wait there."

Whoever had Nicki better pray he didn't find them first, because if she was injured or scared or anything else...he'd become exactly who Victor Pavel trained him to be.

Hanging up his phone, he tossed it into the cup holder before cracking his knuckles. Foot to the floor, he whipped into Castillo's custom-auto paint shop.

Storming through the parking lot, he shoved open the business doors and marched straight into the office. He bypassed all the men working on cars and the others standing guard. The strong solvent fumes, similar to his mom's nail polish remover, added to his pounding headache.

Castillo sat behind a metal desk and looked up from his phone when Erik entered. "Pavel." He nodded in greeting. "I believe I said our business was finished."

"Someone has Nicki."

He lifted his phone and wobbled it back and forth. "I'm aware."

"That doesn't bode well for you, Castillo." Jaw clenched, Erik braced both hands on the desk and leaned forward. "Tell me."

CHAPTER TWENTY-TWO

Nicki lifted her chin when McCord returned. He could break her down. She knew that now. But she'd rise again. She knew that, too. "I 'spose you'll leave her alone now that she doesn't look like your precious Jenny."

The older sister still lay at her feet. She hadn't moved since McCord had last come in, which had likely been about an hour or so.

McCord sat down beside Nicki and pulled a knife from his pocket. A medium-sized Swiss Army knife. He opened it and tilted it back and forth. The blade glistened in the light. "You've been to prison."

She nodded. Hadn't they had this conversation before?

"Did they have any people like me there?"

Nicki considered her answer. She hadn't known any pedophiles, but that wasn't the answer he wanted. "Sure, yeah."

"And how did you treat her?"

"Uh, well, she didn't run with my crew so I don't know."

"Don't lie to me. You know how it is for people like me." He touched the tip of his knife to the little girl's leg. She shivered, but didn't make a sound.

"I know you're looking for a certain answer. You want me to say we beat her up, well I can't say that because we didn't. I was too worried about my own survival in there to worry about anyone else's."

"That's what it's about, right?"

"Survival, I'd say, yeah. Wouldn't want to go back, that's for sure." Actually, she teamed up with some great ladies, and they'd stuck together. No one had really messed with her, but she'd never tell McCord that.

"We survived."

"We did." How much longer that'd be true for her, Nicki couldn't say. She had shot a man after all, and now she was in this spider-infested, freezing-ass basement with a mental patient weirdo who liked playing with knives.

"I've only done one right thing in my life." McCord met her gaze. "One perfect thing. And after all I've been through I should get to have that, shouldn't I? I endured this." He pointed to the scar circling his neck. "I was beaten. They shit and pissed in my cell. My food was taken. I was held down with a knife slicing open my throat until a guard stopped them." He rubbed a hand against his neck for a moment, staring off into space. "And so I deserve to have my Jenny."

"You feel you're justified, I get that." Nicki didn't but none of this conversation would matter with a knife in her heart.

"I don't *feel* anything." He took the tip of the knife and dug it into his palm then held it up to her face. "See. This is nothing. The only time I ever feel is when I see her. When I see my Jenny."

Nicki nodded, because his blood was dripping on the little girl's leg and the smell of the moldy basement and copper was drifting through her nose making her want to gag. This whole talk-your-face-off-before-I-throw-you-in-a-death-pit convo was making her crazy. "And I'll help you get Jenny. Let's go. I'll take the girls somewhere and leave them for a while and bring you Jenny."

He smiled.

Nicki eased back, because that expression was scary, like horror-film-villain scary.

"Yes, that's the plan, but my girls stay here as insurance that you'll return." He pulled a cell phone from his pocket—the kind a person would pick up at a gas station for $19.99 and couldn't be traced.

She shivered at what else he might have in that pocket. *Gross.*

"I'm giving you this phone to call only me. You call the cops, I'll kill them both. You call your lover, Erik Pavel, they're dead. Your friend, Rachel and her ex-cop partner—well, actually, you could invite Clayton along, I have a little payback I'd like to deliver to that man, but you get my meaning."

The whole plan was ridiculous. Of course she'd call for back-up the second he set her free. She wasn't stupid, because if he remained in this creepy basement, how would he know what she was doing?

"Eight hours, that's all you get. You bring me Jenny in eight hours, and we'll make the exchange."

Nicki sucked in her lips then released them with a pop. "I'm sorry, but a wee problem exists with that plan. In order for me to determine where Jenny is, I need to ask the people who know. Clayton certainly being one of them, and he and I aren't exactly the best of friends. So my questions about Jenny will throw up all kinds of red flags, and have him digging into what's happening and so forth. I need a plan B. Sorry." Stall. Delay. Keep McCord occupied with other things besides psychotic haircuts and slicing the skin from her body.

He tapped the tip of the knife against his chin, leaving a tiny smear of blood in the dent.

Her arms ached. Her legs ached. Her face hurt and was all crusty from her crying jag earlier. The girl at her feet was in some sort of mental coma from which she'd likely never return without hours of therapy. Not to mention what might've been done to them before Nicki had arrived. She swallowed down a whole load of bile on that thought.

"You're right, I probably shouldn't let you go."

What? No!

"I'll just send a note somehow. Then you'll go pick up Jenny, and the two girls will remain here until you bring her back to me."

"Um, okay. I get what you're doing here. I get you could kill me. Kill these girls and it's no big thing. I get that. So, I'll do what you ask. I'll..." *Oh, hell make up something quick.* "I'll...I'll rob a bank. I'll shoot a couple people while I'm there to prove I'm serious and tell them they have to bring me Jenny, or I'll murder everyone else. I'll at least get Jenny to the scene before snipers come in and put a bullet in my brain. But you'd be closer to her. She'd come out of hiding, and you could grab her during the chaos. I know Clayton, he'd bring her to the scene. He would. He'd do anything for the greater good. He's got a stupid hero complex, that guy does. Let's do this." She started to sweat, but at the same time her mouth went dry. McCord had to believe her plan. Had to be stupid enough to let her go.

"You're right, Clayton does. And maybe Sheridan would come, too. And she'd cry and beg for people's lives." McCord clapped his hands together and stared at her with wide eyes. "I could wear my cop costume and take Jenny."

"Yes, yes you could. I'd need that phone though, so I could call you once I was in the bank."

"National Trust, just up the road."

"Right, yes." She chewed on her lower lip. "That'd work just as good as any bank."

He nodded. "Just like in the movies."

Of course it was, the whole idea was ridiculous and not at all what she'd do, but mental-patient-McCord didn't know that.

He lifted the girl off the floor and dropped her beside her sister.

Her expression didn't change, which only hardened Nicki's resolve.

"I'll die for you." She told the girls. "You hear me in there? I'm doing this for you. Don't ever think you didn't matter to someone, because you matter to me."

McCord laughed and dropped down beside the sister with the

chopped hair. "You should've seen them. In the gas station all alone. The gallon of milk she was holding was bigger than her. It was easy to drag them off to my car."

Nicki just nodded because all she wanted to do was rip out his throat. Too bad she wouldn't get the chance.

"I'll walk you to the bank."

"What?" Whoa, she hadn't seen that coming, and that made her heart thrum like mad. "My face is basically destroyed. One look at me and everyone will call the cops on you, because they'll assume I'm some battered wife."

"You put too much faith in the human race. No one sees anyone anymore. Our eyes are downcast, living life through social media posts. No one lives in the real world."

Just when she believed him too crazy to fool, he threw down some philosophical shit that made sense. Plus, getting him away from the girls was a good idea.

"All right. I agree."

"Good." He leaned down and kissed each girl's cheek, nuzzling their necks a little.

Nicki fought to breathe, because oh, what a sicko. "Let's go."

"I'll be back soon, my little treats. And I'll have another sister for you. We'll leave here, go someplace else, and have a family."

Nope. Not if she had any say. She studied the room as best she could. No matter what, she had to remember everything. She turned her attention to the girls, took in their clothes, their features. Everything mattered right now.

McCord hauled Nicki to her feet and used the knife to free her wrists. Then bent to cut the rope around her ankles.

Shaking the circulation back into her hands, she briefly considered kneeing him in the face and then kicking him in the nuts. Oh how she wanted to just kick and kick until his nuts were lodged in his stomach. But, if she didn't fully take him down, she knew the consequences would be too horrifying to contemplate.

He gripped her elbow and led her from the room.

A soft cry came from behind her, but she couldn't look back. No, she had to focus straight ahead. After all, she had a bank to rob. And just how would she accomplish that?

CHAPTER TWENTY-THREE

Rubbing her sore wrist, Nicki breathed deeply of the outside air. The sun hit her cheeks, and she didn't think she'd ever felt anything more glorious. She glanced at the giddy man beside her. They stood about a block away from the bank she'd promised to rob. She jarred to a stop, and he bumped into the back of her. "I need a minute."

McCord straightened the collar on the police outfit he'd purchased off the dark web because according to him, "kids trusted cops." Lovely to know these uniforms were available and could be used to commit crimes.

"I'll wait back here." He handed her the flip phone. "Do what you said, or I'll go back and kill them both."

"I heard you already. I just need to think this through for a second." Stall. Stall. Stall. Until she could wave someone down and get rescued.

He'd run a wet washcloth over her face before they'd left, wiping away her snot and tears. Her wrists were a bit raw, and when he'd roughly wiped them off with the same rag he'd just used on her face, she considered all the nastiness that had come out of her nose. She probably shouldn't have fought against the ropes and then she wouldn't be losing her arms at some future date due to some deadly booger infection. She barked out a laugh.

"What's so funny?"

"Just considering all the ways I could die."

"You already said you die in the bank. You said you'd do it so Jenny would come."

Nicki clenched the phone in her hand. *Be smart, Nobles. Talk your way out of this.* "Okay, here's the thing. It's kind of midday and no one is in the bank right now. We need more hostages or this'll never work."

He narrowed his eyes then scanned the parking lot. "Fine."

This small town just outside of Manchester provided the perfect cover for his nasty activities. Hidden in plain sight like every nightmare story she'd ever heard about serial killers. Was he a serial killer? Had he ever killed one of his victims? *Huh.* Why hadn't she thought of this before?

She glanced at the bank and considered if she could make a run for it. If McCord started shooting, maybe she could bob and weave behind some of the trees, lining the sidewalk. Maybe he wouldn't really kill those girls. And maybe she'd throw up in that house's rose bush because she had no idea what she was doing.

The bank was situated on the corner by a two-lane road that led to the highway. A drug store sat across the street. Its parking lot wasn't much busier. They should've waited until people got off work to commit murder and mayhem.

McCord cursed then grabbed her arm.

"Wait." Nicki shook out of her musings and glanced at the man. "What are you doing?"

"We'll come back in an hour. Then regardless of who is here, and who isn't, you're going in." He tugged Nicki back down the street and yanked the phone from her hand.

"Hold on. I'll go now." She jerked to a stop. "Haven't you waited long enough to see Jenny? You're right. I said I do this, and I'm ready." Trying to calm her breathing, she scanned her surroundings looking for someone, anyone, so she could scream. She rocked back and forth on her feet. "Hey, uh...do you have a gun?"

"Why?"

"How am I supposed to rob a bank without a gun?"

He frowned. "I'm not giving you the gun until the last minute. I know all about you shooting Korzakov."

"How do you know that?"

"Everyone knows."

"Then why aren't I dead?"

"I'm sure you will be."

Nicki rubbed a hand against the sting in her wrist again. Sweat trickled down her back, and though starving earlier, she was glad nothing was in her stomach now. "Korzakov isn't relevant to this conversation. We'll walk slowly down the sidewalk. If you're gripping me then people will believe I'm a prisoner or something. They'll be suspicious before we even get within two feet of that bank. So, hands off, okay?"

"Do you think Jenny will like this uniform?"

"What?"

"Jenny." He straightened his shirtsleeve. "She hasn't seen me in a long time. I want to look nice for her."

"Yeah, sure you look great." Nicki sniffed and bit her thumbnail.

"You're just saying that."

Was he serious right now? Her heart was about to explode out of her chest, and all he cared about was a wrinkle in his shirt? "Uh, well, I'm sure she'll be happy to see you no matter what. You are her father, after all." Tossing that out, she hoped to placate him. "But is your shirt buttoned correctly?"

"What?" He glanced down.

"Yeah." She tapped her lip and studied him. "The top one is—"

A car slowed on the road behind McCord and eased toward the curb.

Nicki's swallowed hard. Now was her chance.

"What are you looking at?"

"Squirrel. Just a squirrel." She gripped his arm and kept his attention on her as she checked his buttons with a shaky hand.

He slapped her away. "I'll fix it myself."

"Oh, sorry, I was wrong. They're all good."

"Bitch, are you stalling?"

She glanced over his shoulder. Oh my *God! Raul!* Raul was getting out of the car. How in the hell was he here? A squeak erupted from her throat.

"What do you keep looking at?" McCord spun around then stumbled back a step as he caught sight of Castillo's man. "What are you doing here? Did Korzakov send you?"

Raul nodded and leaned against a tree.

"I was bringing Nicki to him just now."

"Good. He's been looking for her." Raul shot her a wink.

Raul worked for Korzakov? Nicki's hopes of rescue crumbled to dust at her feet. "Y-you...you...and Korzakov." Bad news. So bad. "Raul." She held up a hand. "Okay, okay, just...you can deliver me to Korzakov. I'll go, but listen, McCord's got a couple little girls in there." She pointed at the house. "Please, if you have even a *modicum* of humanity left, save them."

A car came to a stop behind her, but she didn't dare turn around.

The hairs on the back of her neck were scared enough to pop off and make a run for it on their own. No way did she want to turn around and see Korzakov's evil eyes. Wait? Was he still in the hospital? Oh God, what if he was out?

"Shut up, you stupid bitch." McCord lunged for her and then slapped the side of her head. Hard.

She dropped to one knee as a buzzing sound fired through her ear.

McCord yanked her up and dragged her to his side. "She's not going anywhere with you, Raul. I have a job for her, so run along."

A car door slammed shut. Then another.

Please, just shoot me in the head. Put me out of my misery.

Raul looked behind her and grinned before shifting forward.

Oh, sure smile at my death dealers. Hell of a guy, that Raul.

McCord removed a gun from his side holster. "Step back or I'll blow her brains all over this sidewalk."

"That gun come with your outfit?" Likely more than out of her mind, she giggled at that thought. "It's probably fake, Raul. Just shoot him."

"Nicki, stop antagonizing the guy, okay?" Raul arched a dark brow.

"Then let him kill me." Might as well get her death out of the way. Better here than after hours of torture by Korzakov and his men. She'd been held captive by them before, and she'd rather not live that nightmare again. Plus, two frightened girls were in McCord's basement, waiting to be rescued. "Shoot him and get to the girls. No more talking."

"Go ahead and shoot her, McCord." Erik's voice came from behind her. "You'll never see Jenny then, because you'll be dead. And Jenny's right here. I brought her to you. Just step aside."

Nicki blinked then blinked again before shaking her head a little. Was she hallucinating? Was Erik here? Had McCord knocked her brain loose when he'd smacked her?

McCord froze, his strong grip still on her arm. "You're lying."

"Dad." A female voice spoke in hesitant tone.

What? Was Jenny really here?

McCord spun around, dragging Nicki with him.

Rachel Harris leaned against a black car with a cocky smile on her face. "Gotcha."

"No!" McCord sputtered. "Where's Jenny?"

Nicki shoved away from McCord and dodged behind a tree.

A loud pop sounded.

McCord stumbled forward and glanced at his shirt.

Red blossomed.

Another pop, and he fell to the ground.

As he dropped, he fired his gun blindly, over and over.

Nicki held both hands over her ears, body jolting with each bullet fired.

Then it stopped.

Silence.

Entire body shaking, Nicki spared a glance around the tree.

Raul stood over McCord's body, gun in hand.

McCord lifted a hand, reaching for something as he uttered one final word. "Jenny."

CHAPTER TWENTY-FOUR

A lot of what happened between losing Nicki and finding her was still processing in Erik's mind, but basically, Castillo had assigned Raul to watch McCord. Raul had been preparing to storm the pervert's house, but Erik and Rachel had interrupted his rescue. Once they'd arrived, they'd improvised. Rachel throwing out the Jenny card was actually genius, and now McCord was dead. Served him right. Children everywhere were safer now.

Following the standoff, the town cop had arrived, and then the state police. McCord was loaded into a coroner's van and everyone else was hauled to the station except for Nicki. Raul had been the shooter, a role he'd easily confessed. Rachel's uncle, an attorney—and Erik's uncle, too, actually—had hustled in and spoken on their behalf.

Erik and Rachel had arrived at the hospital around the same time as the girls' mother. Nicki had chewed the woman out and then glared at her over the girls' heads while they both waited for the child psychiatrist to arrive. Erik had told Nicki her attitude was upsetting the girls to which he'd received a colorful reply.

So instead of arguing with Nicki over her less-than-helpful behavior, he'd settled into a hard metal seat in the waiting room next to Rachel. It was either that or Nicki was going over his knee for scampering off and getting captured, then having the audacity to give him attitude after he'd risked his life—and his sister's to rescue her. Sure, she hadn't done any of those things on purpose, but his heart hadn't resumed normal activity since seeing her in McCord's clutches. And since he wasn't aware he still had a heart, he had no idea what to think of its existence now.

"So...here we are again." Rachel heaved a long sigh, lifting her short legs straight out and then bumping her toes together.

Shifting in the chair that had lost its cushion eons ago, Erik glanced at his sister. She never sat still, like a hummingbird on crack. Yet her vitality soothed him, and made him grateful they were both alive—and together.

When found, the two little girls had been locked together and shaking as if they were stuck in a hardware store's paint mixer. Seeing them in a heap on the floor with tears pouring down their cheeks was a sight Erik would never forget. They'd screamed when he'd approached, so he and Raul had left Nicki and Rachel to bring them out of the house. The girls had stuck to Nicki like glue. What had they endured? And what about Nicki? What had she seen in that basement?

He didn't have time to contemplate that thought because Raul rounded the corner and came to a stop before them. He wore tan pants and a crisp white dress shirt—an outfit much different from his checkered shirt and jeans at the standoff earlier.

Erik stiffened. The man's whole demeanor seemed different. Not a submissive order-taker for Castillo, but a man sure of his place, legs braced apart, gaze direct, and chin held high. *What the hell?*

"Nicki still in with the girls?" Raul cocked his head back toward the ER area.

Rachel straightened from her slouch beside Erik. "Yes."

Raul nodded and wiped a hand over his cleanly-shaven chin.

"Who do you work for, Raul?" Rachel blurted out the question, oblivious to any undercover situation that might be happening with the man—or maybe just not caring at the moment. Erik had no idea.

Raul turned to Rachel and raised a brow.

Of course, his sister would pick up on the cop vibe. Maybe that came from working with so many of them. Her partner, Clayton was an ex-Manchester detective, after all.

"I work for Castillo." Raul gave a half-shrug then glanced toward the ER's exit.

"Uh-huh."

Raul shook his head before crouching in front of Rachel and meeting her gaze. "I have an appreciation for strong women."

"Okay." Rachel drew out the word, obviously expecting more.

"I respect a woman who can stand her ground in front of a man who's brutalized her in the past."

"So, do I."

"And if that same woman were to commit a crime in order to protect her life, then I would see that as self-defense."

Erik sucked in a breath. The question of whether or not Raul worked for someone besides Castillo was becoming more evident now.

"I agree." Rachel scooted to the edge of her seat, knee bouncing. "The woman, say for example, someone like...Nicki, well, she would be completely justified in shooting at a Russian man who meant her harm. She shouldn't have to endure a trial, go to jail, or even be asked about what she'd done *ever* again."

"Rachel, I don't think..." Erik bit his lip, still unsure which team Raul was playing for, and his sister was asking for a lot on Nicki's behalf.

Raul placed a hand on Rachel's shoulder. "If an official report were to indicate imminent danger existed or say perhaps, a gun simply misfired then I agree that *could* be the case."

"Nicki misfired into Korzakov's face?" Rachel bristled. "Why does it have to be that a *woman* misfired? Not cool."

"Rachel." Erik stilled her bouncing leg. His sister had apparently decided to give up all pretense. "Let it go, please."

Raul grinned and straightened from his crouch.

Erik stood, as well, and held out his hand. "Thank you...for whatever you've done. Nicki is...She wouldn't have let another take the fall for her actions. And I wouldn't have let her go to jail, so...thank you. Again."

Raul shook his hand then clapped Erik on the back. "As I said, I appreciate strong women, and not everything is always so black and white, right?"

"You're playing a very dangerous game."

"We play the game set before us. You know this more than most, yes?"

Erik narrowed his eyes. "Who are you?"

Raul shook his head. "I'm nobody." With a grin, he turned and headed for the door.

"Wait." Erik caught up with him then glanced around, checking to see who was within hearing distance. "So what about the woman Castillo was bringing over from Guerrero?"

"She's here but will be placed elsewhere."

"I'd like to help her financially. Can she be sent back?"

"No."

"That woman was brought over to protect mine. I want to know she's safe."

"She is." Raul stepped closer, steel in his gaze. "Do not make any inquiries into the Guerrero woman's whereabouts. Keep your focus on Nicki. And just so you know, Nicki said nothing happened. With McCord."

"You asked her. McCord...he didn't..."

"I was in the...vicinity when Nicki was questioned."

"Korzakov isn't dead. She's still in danger, regardless of who you are or the reports you've made."

"He's over. Nothing he scrabbles together can save him. One way or the other he's finished." Raul kept Erik's gaze for a moment before nodding and then he sauntered toward the exit.

Having no idea what that meant, especially since Korzakov was still in a coma, Erik simply watched Raul walk away.

"Whoa. I didn't see that coming."

Rachel's exclamation brought Erik's attention back to the present and halted all the questions flying through his mind.

She took his hand. "It's going to be okay. I don't know why, but I feel like that was the last thing."

He didn't agree but he didn't pull away either, because her grip felt kind of nice. And he'd blame that bit of sappiness on seeing the two redheaded sisters clutching each other for comfort. Over and over, he'd tried to convince himself Rachel didn't matter, but that had never been true. Whether he liked it or not, once again, *they* were huddled together, having survived another harrowing moment in their lives.

And that was how he'd continue, one moment at a time. "The last thing is Korzakov in a cold grave." Erik huffed out a sigh. "I don't want to talk about Raul and whatever the hell it is he's doing."

"All right. Probably best to keep all that on the down-low anyway."

"I'll have to tell Nicki."

"Yes." Rachel led him back to their seats.

"She'll need a friend."

Rachel nodded. "Yes, she will." She shoved him into the seat then sat beside him. "I imagine she might need a bit of love, too. I'm going to leave that part to you, though. I know she's bisexual, but I'm good with Bronco. He may fantasize about a three-way with another woman, but that ain't happening on my watch."

"That's a really disturbing visual, Rach." Erik glared at her, trying not to smile when she just winked.

"Earlier, before all the craziness happened, you said she was leaving, did you mean like leaving leaving? And if so, are you...uh...will you go, too?"

"I don't know. I may not be able to leave during the investigation into McCord's death, but sometime, yeah, I get why she wants to go. Lots of dark memories here. Maybe with Raul being whoever he is, this McCord case will be wrapped up quickly."

"Could be." Rachel nodded and grabbed his hand again. Eyes downcast as she played with his fingers. "But you didn't really answer my question, will you go away? Together?"

"No, not together." At least he didn't think so. Today had rocked his world. He'd almost lost Nicki, and panic was too small a word for the foreign emotions ripping through his chest. Normally, when facing danger, he remained calm and handled each issue with ruthless efficiency. But not today. Not with Nicki. What was he supposed to do with all this chaos buzzing around in his brain? If this was what caring for someone felt like, he wasn't sure he wanted it.

"Erik?" Rachel bumped his shoulder.

"Yeah."

"I said, I think a move would be good for both of you. You're both like, blah, blah, blah, no one can ever love me 'cause I'm a bad person." She rolled her eyes. "It's horse-hockey. I'd know because I spouted that nonsense before I got tamed by the mammoth cock-monster."

"Again, not a visual I need." Erik pulled away his hand.

She grabbed it again. "All right, I'll change the subject. Your poor car. McCord really shot it up, didn't he?"

He shrugged. Better his car than her or Nicki. When McCord had fired wildly while on the ground bleeding to death, Erik had tackled Rachel into a yard.

"I'll miss this." Rachel squeezed his hand.

"What? Hanging out in hospital rooms after being shot at?"

"No, Erik." She sighed. "You know what I mean when I say I'll miss this. I'll miss you if you go away with Nicki."

That shocked him, because he'd never been kind to her, so what would she miss? He nodded, and luckily Nicki emerged from the corridor, because he didn't know what to say.

Nicki stormed over, her expression fierce. "I don't want my girls to stay with that woman. I'll take them and disappear if I have to. She doesn't deserve them." She wiped at a tear on her cheek. "I've *been* them, and I can't leave them with their drug-addict mother. She was in a bar!" Nicki paced back and forth. "Her kids are missing and she's drunk and high in a bar. Who does that? I wanted to rip out her throat."

Erik shot to his feet and took her hand. "We'll take care of it."

"I'm so angry."

"I know." Her whole body practically vibrated. Likely she was on edge after everything that had happened and was focusing her anger on the mother of the two girls. The fire in her eyes and the flush on her cheeks had him thinking of other ways to alleviate her stress. And not just sweaty sex, but holding her in his arms until she felt safe again.

Nicki blinked before taking a deep breath. "I think...I think I want them."

"What?"

"I want them to live with me."

"Nicki, you can't afford to take care of two kids. Not only that, you can't just take them from their mother."

"I can and I will."

He turned and met Rachel's gaze.

She nodded as if she had some secret plan. Then she stood, too. "Well then, let's talk to Uncle Harris and see what we can start. Bronco and I will help."

"Rachel, I don't want your charity."

"I just dodged bullets for you. You're not charity, you're family, so shut your face."

Nicki's lower lip started to wobble then she basically leapt into Rachel's arms and burst into tears.

He wasn't sure Nicki's plan would work, or even if her plan was such a great idea, but he understood her need to aid those two girls.

Unable to bear the wracking sobs pouring from his strong and independent woman, he eased Rachel away and wrapped Nicki in his arms. He stroked her hair and whispered words of comfort. Nothing he said made sense, but that didn't matter right now.

Rachel wormed her way between them and wrapped her arms around them both.

Apparently, he couldn't escape Nicki or Rachel. And maybe for once in his life he didn't want to. Maybe this was what he'd sought all along. An answer. An end. A family. And didn't endings sometimes also spark beginnings? He ran his fingers through Nicki's silky black hair. He could have her. He certainly wanted her. But could he convince her to begin again—with him?

CHAPTER TWENTY-FIVE

Erik flipped on the light switch and led Nicki to the living room. The apartment building and the hallways were fitted with state of the art security, so Erik felt safe here. Nicki had agreed to accompany him, likely because she was too tired to argue or perhaps still shell-shocked from her abduction. Though she *had* been cleared-headed enough to garner a promise from Rachel to speak to their uncle about the girls.

He drew Nicki to the plush leather couch. "I need to shower. Why don't you do the same?" Maybe she'd feel better if she washed away some of the filth and death from today. He still didn't know what McCord had done, but after spending any time with the vile man he'd always felt better standing under a hot stream of cleansing water. Not everything escaped down the drain, but the symbolism of the action generally cleared his head.

"In...in a separate bathroom?"

Her tone seemed hesitant, and her gaze darted around the room. *What is she looking for?* His heart ached for all she'd been through. "Yes, separate bathrooms. You need some space, right?"

"I do, but I don't." Nicki rubbed her hands up and down her arms. "Where are your towels and stuff?"

"Are you cold? A shower will warm you up." Erik tugged her to her feet and wrapped her in his arms. She didn't smell like bubble gum, but instead like an old musty basement. He squeezed her tighter. "It'll be okay now."

"How's that?"

"For one, you're alive." He eased back and kissed her chilled forehead. "The other is you won't be charged with shooting Korzakov."

Her brow furrowed. "I already said I don't want that." She shoved away. "I shot him and no one else can—"

He pressed a finger against her lips. "Hey, listen for a second."

"What?" She braced both hands on her hips.

"Raul took care of it."

"Took care of it?" Cocking her head to the side, Nicki tapped a finger against her chin. "How's that?"

"I don't really know."

"Well that clarifies everything." She threw her hands in the air and stormed down the hallway. "I'm hogging all the hot water, Pavel. You're shit out of luck if you planned to shower tonight."

A door slammed shut.

Grinning, he settled back onto the couch and clicked on the news. Seeing the fire in her eyes, regardless if the fury was aimed at him was better than her defeated slouch. He shifted his rock hard dick. Damn the woman was sexy as hell when in a rage.

"Wait."

He shot around, hand reaching for his gun—which he wasn't carrying. "Jesus, you startled me."

"Quit shrieking like a girl." Nicki rolled her eyes. "If Raul is doing whatever he's doing to cover my Korzakov shooting then what will Castillo do about that woman who was supposed to take my place?"

"Raul said she's being taken care of."

Nicki's eyes went wide. "Wha...What?"

"No." Erik stood and rounded the couch. "He's not killing her. He said she was being provided for, and I believe him."

Nicki shook her head then stared up at the ceiling. "Why? Why me?" She rubbed her eyes. "You know what, I'm good. Okay. I'll just chalk that up to one less thing to worry about, because I can't right now." She cruised back down the hall, mumbling to herself.

"Nicki."

She stopped but didn't turn around.

"When you're ready to talk about what happened, I'm here."

She nodded and continued down the hall.

After a jaw-cracking yawn, Erik headed toward his own bathroom and then checked his phone while waiting for the water to heat. He'd sent Clayton a text while at the hospital, giving the all clear. Jenny was safe now that McCord was dead and maybe some of Sheridan's demons could be laid to rest, too. He hadn't heard back from them, but Clayton was likely in the thick of things down at the police station. The ex-Manchester detective would know every detail of the shooting by now, and he'd come knocking on Erik's door to get his version of events soon enough.

After showering, Erik tossed on black sweats and a long-sleeved cotton shirt. Sitting on the couch, he sipped a beer, wondering if this was one of those moments better served with a glass of expensive whisky—something that would soothe or calm him, because his mind was reeling.

Nicki tiptoed out, wrapped in a fluffy navy blue towel. "I don't have anything to wear."

"I left you a T-shirt on the spare bedroom's bed." Since he bought extra tall shirts, he'd figured it'd be long enough to cover her essentials.

"All right." She turned and plodded back down the hall.

Too much of her spunk was gone again. They needed to talk, but asking about feelings wasn't his forte. Although, considering the whole idea of feelings, he knew he'd already succumbed to the inevitable. He wanted Nicki and she wanted him, and they were working on this relationship tonight. He was a bad bet, but he believed they could cobble together a relationship. Start over together somewhere else. He'd actually warmed to the idea.

Korzakov was still in the hospital, and if he survived, then being out of town with different identities was best. Maybe US Marshal Leonard could give them access to a secure location for a time. He'd hear from the man soon due to McCord's shooting, and Erik would ask for help then.

"Oh, good. You're drinking." Nicki sauntered back into the room, hair wet, cheeks flushed, face bruised and her wrists a bit red.

"I am." He let his gaze drift up her long legs. "I was just lamenting over the fact I don't have anything stronger."

"The world needs an alcohol delivery system like pizza, because sometimes you have an I-need-to-get-drunk-right-now emergency."

"Good idea. We'll start it together. What should we call this alcohol delivery business?"

Nicki set a throw blanket on the leather couch and sat beside him. "Um...how about...Oh, I know, Whino Call?"

"Booze-to-Yooz."

She chuckled "We could totally start this business. We'd make a fortune."

"What happened to you in that basement?"

"Whoa." She held up her hand. "Abrupt subject change."

Interrogation tactics were something Erik had learned by watching Pavel. Of course, Pavel's questions were generally delivered with a bullet to the thigh or a crunch of a finger. That wasn't such a good idea here, so Erik tugged on a loose strand of Nicki's hair instead. "Tell me."

She pursed her lips then sniffed. "I'll just say it was worse than the time I was nine and this man held me down and tried to shove a coke bottle in my mouth, because I wouldn't shove his something else in there."

Deflection, something she was good at, and he'd play, just once. "That's not as bad as the time Pavel stabbed this guy in the heart, had him bleed out in a bathtub, and made me clean the tub after."

"Huh, that's pretty wicked." Nicki flicked her hair over her shoulder. "But still doesn't top the time my Mom got high on acid and dropped me off in the woods near our house. At one in the morning, she just left me there. I had to walk home, wearing only socks and pajamas. It was late fall, too. I froze my little buns off and about peed my pants every time I heard something skitter around me."

Heart aching for that scared little girl, he took Nicki's hand. Who else could he have these conversations with? No one. That had to mean something, and he wanted to discover what that was. "Everything I've ever said to you is true."

"Did I ever say I was lying?" She huffed out a half-laugh and wrapped the black chenille throw blanket over her legs.

"What happened in that basement?"

She shrugged and her gaze drifted to her fingers, which were running along the fuzzy edge of the blanket. "You saw those girls."

"I did." He drew her to his side then kissed the top of her head. She smelled like his shampoo, and his feral side enjoyed the fact she was marked with his scent. "Tell me."

Quiet for a moment, she shuffled back against him and then spoke in a soft, barely audible tone. "McCord cut her hair. He held her down and cut it, and I just screamed. I couldn't do anything." With a low growl, she shot up off the couch, tossing the blanket on the floor. "I hate feeling helpless." She paced in front of him, her long legs stomping back and forth. "I had no idea what he would do to them, and I knew...I knew I'd have to see it. And that thought...it broke me. He broke me." She raked a shaky hand through her damp hair. "I mean, I've been in hell before, but what McCord did was different. Sickening and so depraved. I-I still feel like his evil has sunken into me somehow."

Erik stood and gripped her shoulders. "I understand."

"I know." Her shoulders drooped. "Out of anyone I know you do."

"That's right."

"What's right?" She frowned.

"I know you, and you know me, and we both know what that means." He gripped the back of her neck and tugged her against his chest. "McCord had a gun to your head, and I caught a glimpse of everything that would disappear if you weren't with me. I didn't like it." He pressed a kiss to her temple. "I've lived for revenge, but I want to live for something else now. I want to live for you and me." He held Nicki tighter when she tried to pull away. "I'll never forget my mom. Never. But you, and yes, Rachel were right about so many things, and I need you to show me how to live differently. You may not need me, but we don't have a choice anymore. I won't give you a choice."

She pressed a hand against his chest. "There's always a choice."

He arched a brow. "And I explained what that *will* be."

"Cocky aren't you." She grinned up at him.

"So are you."

"When wooing a woman, a man should flatter her, not tell her she's cocky, or how she'll live the rest of her life."

He bumped her hips with his. "I like it when you say cocky."

Her eyes widened and she shoved two knuckles against this chest. "Oh my God, who are you right now?"

"A man who wants to fuck you. Who *will* fuck you."

"Holy shit. You...you...what?"

"Since you can't form coherent sentences, I'll find another use for your mouth." He cupped her cheek, hauled her against his body, and then looked for the slightest hint of reserve.

She licked her lips.

So he dove, into her—and their future.

NICKI BACKED up against the King size bed. They'd somehow worked their way to the bedroom, kissing and tugging off clothes.

Naked now, she moaned as Erik dropped wet kisses down her neck before dipping and latching on to her nipple. Her hips arched, as if they'd decided on their own that this was a good idea. And after all she'd been through, why not? McCord could have killed her in that basement, so she'd take this moment and revel in being alive. For a short time in her life, sex had been about getting the job done and keeping the customer satisfied, but not this. Not now.

This was Erik's body against hers. This was her choice. This was heat and fire, and everything she'd craved for so long. This was about getting a piece of the one man who could understand her like no other. And by the way his lips, tongue, and mouth worked over her body, he understood her body as much as her heart. An undeniable connection roared between them, making her pant and fight to breathe.

She needed him to wipe away the past couple days ugliness. But not only that, she simply needed *him*, a fact becoming more and more clear each time they were together. What they had wasn't something she could fight anymore, so she'd release it all.

"Make me forget. Please, Erik." She tugged him down for a dirty kiss, all teeth and tongues. Easing back, she cupped his warm ball sac. "You said you were going to fuck me, and that's exactly what I want. Take me."

"We'll fuck the first time then take it slow the second." Erik lifted off her body, and then stood at the side of the bed.

"What are you doing?" Her heels dug into the mattress and she reached for him. "It's cold without you."

Grinning, he flipped her over and smacked her ass. "Get up and bend over the side of bed."

"You could say please, you know." She arched a brow, but complied, because she wanted his thick cock in her *now*.

Seemingly determined to make her crazy with lust, he turned and grabbed supplies out of his side table.

Bent over, with her arms braced on the bed, she glanced over her shoulder, taking a moment to peruse his fine form. Muscled thighs, chest lightly-dusted, a divine happy trail centered between clearly-defined Adonis muscles. Holy fuck, she couldn't wait to feel all that banging against her ass.

Her core ached, and her pussy was practically drooling at the site of his body.

Yet for some reason, he continued to stand there rubbing his leaking cockhead. Her mouth watered for a taste, and she licked her lips. "What's the hold up, Pavel?" She wiggled her ass. "I already heard you open the condom, so get that dick in me."

Strong arms banded around her waist and caressed their way up to her breasts. "Not this time."

"What?"

"I want to play with you a little."

She groaned and dropped her forehead against the bed. "We said a hard fucking first *then* we'll take our time. I'm about to come just thinking about your dick buried deep inside my wet pussy. I want to feel your hot sac slapping against my ass. I want you to own me, and ride me hard." She bit her bottom lip. "Is all my dirty talk working? Can we fuck now, please?"

"Damn it. You know it is." He slapped her bottom again then pressed his dick between her ass cheeks, sliding the wet head up and down. "This what you want?" He dipped his fingers inside her wet core, thrusting them in and out.

"No." Nicki scooted up the bed, and just the press of her breasts against the sheets had her body pulsing with far too many sensations. "I want you. Please, Erik."

He chuckled. "We'll get to that. You're not in charge here, Nobles. I am." He pinched her ass cheek then dropped to his knees behind her. Then he licked a swath from her throbbing clit to her ass. Using both hands, he held her ass cheeks apart as he pressed the flat of his tongue against her puckered whole, circling around the tender flesh.

"You're a dirty mother fucker. That's so nasty but I love it." She hissed and ran her fingers over her nipples, plucking and teasing them as he slid two fingers into her wet core. Dying to come, she rubbed her mound against the bed.

"What are you doing?" He yanked her hips up, and then attacked the side of her neck with hot, wet kisses.

She tilted her head to the side. "I was trying to get enough friction to come, you jerk."

He reached around her body and pressed his fingers against her clit. "Is this enough friction?"

Close to the edge, she whimpered, squeezing her nipples hard, before flicking them with her thumbs. "Perfect friction. Don't stop."

Brushing her hair over her shoulder, he kissed and bit her neck while at the same time hitting the perfect spot to push her over the edge.

Spasms wracked her body, and she bent over from their intensity. Her empty core pulsed over and over, seeming to beg for more, even after this amazing moment of bliss.

Still lost to pleasure, Nicki fought to catch her breath as he rubbed his wet fingers along her mouth. "Taste your pleasure."

She laved her tongue around his fingers, tasting herself and wishing it was his cum coating her lips instead.

Flipping her body, he settled her ass on the edge of the bed and nudged open her thighs. And then he plunged. Deep, so deep, slamming into her core.

"Oh, fuck yes." Her eyes flew open. Her lethargic body awakening again at this plunder.

Erik's dark brown eyes were heavily hooded and locked at where they were joined together.

He grabbed her hand and pressed it against her overly sensitive core. "Touch yourself until you come."

Dominant Erik was hot. Keeping her gaze on him, she detoured across her breasts before fingering her aching mound.

He halted his driving thrusts and shoved her further up the bed, following behind, before spreading her open and entering her again with a single lunge. Setting a driving pace, he bent to kiss her, working his tongue into her mouth, owning her, and taking her to a place she'd never been before.

She gasped, as her body still floated high from her last orgasm, the sensations of this forceful fucking almost too much to bear.

He released her mouth, his lips deep red and damp. Then he brought his fingers to her mouth. "Suck on them."

Erik had a taste-kink apparently. She did as he asked, biting and nipping at his fingers, drawing them deep in her mouth and moaning around them.

"That's my dirty girl. Now come for me."

She bit down hard on his thumb, pressed her fingers against her clit, and exploded around his cock. Panting for breath, she closed her eyes and drifted on wave after wave of pleasure. His finger still in her mouth, she sucked hard as tiny bursts twitched through her core. "Holy fuck," she mumbled as he pulled his fingers from her mouth.

He leaned over her body, grinning, with sweat trickling down the side of his face.

She'd remember that look of satisfaction in his eyes forever. She sighed and closed her eyes.

"Hey, we're not done yet?" Erik shook her shoulder.

"We aren't?" Eyes drifting closed again, she barely lifted her arm off the bed to wrap around his shoulders. The room smelled like sex and sweat and everything divine.

"Nope, it's your turn to work."

"What?" Her eyes shot open. "I'm tapping out."

With a chuckled, he turned onto his back and dragged her body on top of his. "Ride me."

His lusty murmur vibrated across her lower portions, which had her rising to the occasion again. "I wasn't prepared to get in the saddle today. You shouldn't wear a girl out then tell her to hop on." Lusciously sore, she straddled him, fitting his thickly veined cock deep inside her once more. "Damn, Pavel. Your dick is practically purple."

"Had to make sure you were satisfied before I took my own."

"Such a gentleman." Rising up and down, Nicki gripped his

shoulders for support. "And, I'm very, very satisfied, but let's see if we can take this just a little higher."

"I'd bet on you any day." Erik rose up to kiss her breasts, and then bit at her nipples.

Rolling her hips against him, she couldn't stave off the orgasm that quickly built. Too many pleasurable sensations tingled and only needed a modicum of stimulation to explode once more.

He wrapped his hands in the hair at the back of her neck and tugged. "Look at me as I come. See what you do to me," he gasped, licking his bottom lip. "Only you."

She kept his gaze, loving the twinge of pain from his tight grip on her hair. One more time, she could reach that peak one more time.

He lowered back onto the bed and gripped her hips. He rocked up each time she plunged down, over and over, faster and faster until pleasure barreled through her.

He stilled, and the cords on his neck stood out as he gritted his teeth and released a long, low moan. His entire body shuddered, and his head practically dented the pillow.

Seeing him come undone, pushed her own release even higher. She may have even blacked out for a moment before she collapsed on his chest.

"So hot." His words came out like a growl. "Damn, woman." He trailed his fingers along her slick skin, dancing along her spine until she shivered.

"Mmm..hmm." Crumbling onto her side, she pressed her thighs together, trying to quell the lingering spasms rocketing through her core. "That's some stamina, Pavel. You fucked me good. Go team." Barely awake, she waved a limp wrist in the air. "Way to score that goal...or whatever."

He chuckled and then moved her body as if she were a rag doll until she rested against his chest. "Wasn't easy. That's why I started from behind but even that was a miscalculation. You have a very nice ass, Ms. Nobles."

She grunted, unsure what to do next, even what to think next.

Was he telling the truth earlier about wanting more with her? Sex was more, sure, but what else? And why wouldn't her mind shut off even when her body said, lights out, bitch.

He ran his fingers through her hair. "What's wrong?"

"What could possibly be wrong? I just had three mind-blowing orgasms."

"This is true."

She flicked a hand against his chest due to his smug tone. "It's just..."

"What?"

And though Nicki didn't want to ruin the moment, she had to get this off her chest. "If we're going to do this thing, then I want a proper build up. We had all this fear, and worry, and general craziness, but I want to see what happens when we just do normal. Go on dates... things like that." If she was placing her heart in Pavel's hands, then she wanted romance. No half-measures. She'd never thought to have someone who'd understand her, so she'd take advantage of the situation and succumb to the fairytale.

Erik yawned and stretched his long body beside hers. "We still need to leave. Start over. I'm surprised Leonard isn't beating down my door. He will, and when he does, I'll ask for his help. We'll have to lie low until Raul whoever-he-is finalizes everything. We have a little time since Korzakov is still in the hospital."

"Is he still critical?" She shivered and snuggled closer to Erik.

"Yes."

Erik ran a finger across Nicki's shoulder. "I need you to understand that if we leave, we won't be able to take the sisters."

In order to see his face, she folded her hands on his chest and then rested her chin on top. "I don't know about that. They need me, and not just because of McCord's disgusting actions. I recognize all the signs of neglect, and I can't walk away. I don't know what to do though...not really. I mean they love their mom, but she's messed up."

"We'll figure it out." He brushed her hair out of her eyes. "Once a decision is made, we'll help them, one way or another."

"Okay."

"Okay? That's all you have to say?"

She shrugged then fiddled with the hairs on his chest. "I'm sure about helping the girls, but I'm still not so sure about you and me."

"How can I further convince you?" He trailed a finger down her cheek and nudged her with his hips.

Nicki trailed a hand down his body and gripped his thick cock. A second wind was blowing in from somewhere—blowing being the operative word. "You can convince me in the shower, then persuade me across the bathroom counter top, then I might even let you encourage me back here in bed. How's that sound?"

"Ambitious. I like it."

She kissed him hard and then smacked the side of his thigh even harder. "Keep up, Pavel. I have no problem taking what I want." That said, she bolted out of bed and sashayed toward the bathroom.

"Neither do I." Erik yanked on her arm, tossed her back on the bed then sprawled across her body before wedging open her thighs. "You ready?"

She met his gaze, aware his question meant so much more. Placing her hand against his scruffy cheek, she nodded and left behind every doubt clogging her mind. "I'm ready."

CHAPTER TWENTY-SIX

Two weeks later, just after midnight, Erik sat across the booth from Nicki and smiled as Sarah dropped off their pancakes, along with a mound of bacon. He'd brought Nicki to the diner to close a chapter. His mother had brought him here to escape the real world, and he wanted to share this piece of his past with Nicki. His mother would've approved of Nicki's vitality, and her I'm-okay-alone-but-I'll-let-you-in view on life.

After talking with Leonard, they'd been informed they couldn't leave town yet due to the McCord's shooting. Remaining here made Erik twitchy, but Leonard had explained that, as usual, they'd have a few men keeping an eye on him.

Korzakov's empire had fallen, and Castillo had taken over his territories. Erik didn't want to know what had been done to make that happen. Korzakov continued his stay in a private hospital room under guard by federal agents. The authorities were finally able to arrest him with all the information given by his accountant and other "anonymous" sources.

During the first week after the McCord incident, he and Nicki had fought pretty hard over her independent nature and her desire to go back to work. She had a hard time comprehending they weren't out of the woods yet. They might not ever be. Once Korzakov was out of the hospital and in jail, and when McCord's trial was over, they'd move to Florida. Nicki still visited the little sisters every day, and their mom seemed to be turning over a new leaf. Erik had paid to move them into a new apartment and worked with his connections to get her a better job. They had to be satisfied with that for now.

Pouring syrup over her pancakes, Nicki hummed low in her throat. A sound that grabbed Erik's attention—and his dick's. He grinned over her breakfast-ecstasy. "Should I be jealous?"

"These pancakes are amazing. And bacon!" Nicki grabbed a piece and stuffed it in her mouth. "Crispy, just the way I like it."

"I can understand why you're so hungry." He grinned when she blushed. They'd worked up quite an appetite before coming to the diner.

She kicked him under the table. "Shut it."

More than ready to get her back to his bed, he dug into his pancakes. "Should I leave you alone with your bacon?"

Narrowing her eyes, she slid the plate closer to her. "Yes. I'm having a moment."

"Didn't you have one earlier?"

"I did, and after you're rejuvenated, I will again."

"Is that right?"

"It is." She nodded, her expression quite serious.

He laughed, loving that she was just as insatiable as him. Shaking his head, he grabbed his coffee. Just before the glass touched his bottom lip, he heard the bells jangle on the café's door. Glancing up from his position in the back booth, he caught site of Leonard.

The Marshal strode forward with a frown on his face, and he kept darting glances out the windows.

Erik's dropped his fork and reached for the gun hidden under his jacket. "What is it?"

"Korzakov escaped."

Shouting a curse, Erik shot to his feet. "He was in a *coma*."

"No, he wasn't."

"Explain," Erik barked.

Leonard shifted the cowboy hat on his head. "He paid a doctor and a nurse to say he was incapacitated, but he was lucid and healing the whole time."

"The *whole* time?"

"Yes."

Erik grabbed Leonard by his shirtfront. "And you never thought to question these doctors? Never brought in your own people to check Korzakov's condition?"

Leonard grabbed Erik's wrists. "Not relevant now. We need to get you out of here and to a more secure location."

"What about the guards at the hospital?"

"Dead."

Erik gritted his teeth and stared down at Nicki.

Her eyes were wide, but she reached over and placed a hand on Erik's arm. "Can I take the bacon?"

How could she worry about bacon when they were in extreme danger? "Nicki, this isn't a joke. Korzakov's got something to prove to his brigade now. He will do anything to reassert his position. I know, because it's what I'd do. Killing you and me and everyone we know is on his to-do list." He rubbed his forehead. "God damn it! I can't believe he tricked us all. I knew we should've just left town. Fuck!"

Leonard shot him a glance before he tugged Nicki from her seat. "Erik's right. Let's go. Sorry about your bacon."

On their way to the door, Erik jerked as the glass windows exploded, shooting fine bits across the floor and piercing his skin. He spun around. "Nicki!"

Leonard had already hauled her to the floor.

"I hope you brought backup." Erik cocked his gun and crouched down, searching for better cover.

"Sorry, kid. I didn't trust anyone else."

"That's just great, Leonard." Heart racing, Erik heard Sarah and the employees yelling and screaming in the kitchen. "Sarah, get out of here. Go out the back if you can!" Erik stayed low and hollered at Leonard, "I've got eight rounds in my .45. What've you got?"

"Seven in the magazine and one in the chamber."

"Damn it."

"Always knew you'd be the death of me, kid." Leonard gripped Erik's shoulder and squeezed before crawling behind the diner's counter.

Erik pulled Nicki forward, following Leonard to the only available cover for their last stand. Once in place, Erik tipped up her chin with his index finger. "I'm sorry."

She bit her bottom lip. "Just shoot the fuckers. It's because of them, I'm missing out on bacon."

Erik shook his head. "So, we're ending this with bacon?"

"Oh, I'm sorry. Were we supposed to declare our love for each other before we get bullets in our brains?"

"I think so, yes." He brushed her hair behind her ear.

She sucked in a breath then released it before bracing a hand against his cheek. "Fine then, yeah, I might love you a little. I hate you most of the time, but loving you is a lot better than anything I've ever known. I've never had much in my life, and if I only get these past two weeks with you, then...well, that'll have to be enough."

Erik closed his eyes for a moment, because any second now, no matter how many rounds he fired, he knew they were outgunned, outmanned, and would die. He met her gaze again. "Go out the back. Escape if you can."

"Erik, please." A plea for something more was in her eyes.

"Okay, yes, if this horrible feeling in my chest right now is love, then yes, I guess I love you, too."

"You do?" Tears formed in her eyes and spilled over.

"It *is* nice to say it just once."

"So you're just *saying* it?" She punched his shoulder.

Car doors slammed shut outside the diner, but he didn't let her go.

The clank of the bells sounded against the door again.

The crunch of feet against glass.

This was it, his last chance to tell her how he felt. "I'm not just saying the words, Nicki. I'm feeling it, too." Erik pulled her close and kissed her. "Thank you...for all of it. For forgiving me. For loving me. For everything I never thought I'd have."

"You say all this now!" Nicki shrieked.

"Yeah, better late than never, right?"

"Right." She visibly swallowed and then tapped his nose with her finger. "For bacon?"

"For bacon." He nodded. "Leonard, we doing this?"

Leonard shot him a grin. "The only way to go."

"Damn straight." Erik rose from his position, aimed at the big ass man standing beside Korzakov, and fired off a round.

Leonard did the same.

Then they both ducked.

A barrage of bullets rained down on their heads.

Erik covered Nicki with his body. "Baby, get out of here." He tried shoving her toward the kitchen doors, but she wouldn't move. "God damn it, woman!" Couldn't she hear him? Why wouldn't she leave?

Glass dishes broke as round after round of gunfire was returned.

Ketchup splattered.

Sugar spilled.

The splintered coffee pots dripped hot black liquid down the counter's side.

Leonard shouted something, but Erik couldn't make out his words over the gunfire.

With a roar, Erik rose up again, fired, but then a sharp pain burst in his shoulder and blasted him against the counter.

Nicki screamed.

Korzakov's man, Yegor stalked forward.

Leonard stood, fired off a few rounds, and then crumbled to the ground, red blooming on his right shoulder. He cursed then plastered his phone to his ear, yelling at someone.

And then *his* voice sounded with a shout, breaking through all the chaos. "Enough!"

Erik pressed Nicki into the back counter, knocking over a stack of coffee cups.

The shattering glass filled the silence.

His shoulder ached. His hearing was muffled. Sweat trickled down his back.

Nicki squeezed his hand.

He turned and met her gaze.

She grinned, and wiped at the tears on her cheeks. Her mouth formed the words, "I love you."

Pulling from that love, he pushed away any sorrow over the fact that she'd die, and he'd die, and their love would simply end. She didn't deserve this. Him, yes. Her, never. But he wouldn't regret their time together, not when he was huddled beside her. They'd each given the other a short glimpse at a different life, and for them, those stolen moments would have to be enough.

Shaking his head, he gave her a wink.

She winked back.

After taking the only goodbye they would get, he passed his gaze over the café. A place that had been a safe haven was now destroyed. Tables were overturned. Glass was everywhere. A saltshaker spilled onto the floor.

Three of Korzakov's men moaned on the floor, bleeding from various bullet wounds. Somehow Erik had been able to hit his target or maybe that sharp shooting could be laid at Leonard's door. Didn't matter. They were both out of bullets.

Four more men stood beside Korzakov.

"Are you done?" Korzakov stepped forward, a revolver in his hand.

Gritting his teeth, Erik pressed a hand against his bloody shoulder. "Depends on what else you got."

"Oh, I've got plenty, and *you* are out of bullets." Korzakov sniffed then jerked his head toward the counter. "Get the girl."

Erik waited until the men rounded the counter before opening his arms, belting out a battle cry, and charging forward. Punching, dodging, and kicking, he took down two, but an upper cut by Yegor had him seeing stars. He shook off the blow. Blood dripped from his nose and his bottom lip. He could barely see out of his right eye. The copper flavor filling his mouth seemed the bitter taste of defeat. He stumbled but lifted his arms again, blocking his face from the multitude of blows.

Where the fuck had Leonard gone?

Nicki shouted a round of colorful obscenities.

Two men had worked their way around the counter and grabbed her.

But she fought.

And seeing her in their clutches had him fighting with everything he had left. But another blow to the side of his head dropped him to his knees.

"Erik." Nicki screamed, but with two men gripping her arms, she couldn't do much more than wiggle and kick.

Blinking through the sweat pouring down his face and his battered eye, Erik struggled to his feet, only to be rewarded for his efforts with a swift kick to his ribs.

Pain spiking through his body, he clutched his waist and searched for Nicki.

Two men held her at Korzakov's feet.

This tableau all too familiar.

A nightmare.

Just like his mother.

Please, not again.

Korzakov met Erik's gaze and grinned. "Here we are once again. I was going to kill you, but I think I'll leave you behind. Why should you receive an end to your suffering? And this is just the start. Your sister is next."

Korzakov pointed the gun at Nicki's chest.

"No." Voice raw, Erik tried to shove forward but beefy arms held him back.

Vehicles with flashing lights roared to a stop just beyond the shattered windows. Everyone glanced that way, but Korzakov's gaze stayed on Erik's.

Leonard hobbled out of the kitchen, gun aimed at Korzakov. "Let her go. You're surrounded."

"You've got nothing left."

"You sure about that?"

Korzakov grinned and leveled the gun at Nicki again.

Several gunshots went off at once.

The men holding Erik dropped to their knees, taking him down with them.

Erik was trapped under two big bodies. He closed his eyes. He couldn't move. Couldn't look. Not again. He'd failed. Lost a woman he loved.

Someone shook his wounded shoulder. He winced but reveled in the pain, because didn't he deserve it?

"Erik? You still with me?" Someone shouted in his face, jostling him free of the dead bodies.

He opened his eyes to see Raul peering down at him. "Where's Nicki?"

Raul shook his head. "The EMTs are here."

"Meaning what?" Heart pounding, Erik scrambled to his feet and rounded the counter, slipping on the greasy—and bloody floor.

Sirens blared but the sound was slightly muffled. Ears ringing, he wiped at the sweat on his face, and blinked open his one good eye, breathing past the pain in order to find Nicki.

Yegor was dead.

Raul was shirtless, having wadded up the fabric to press against Leonard's wounded side. They were speaking to one another but Erik couldn't make out the words.

Where was Nicki?

In the carnage of the diner, he couldn't see her.

Bodies lay strewn across broken tables. The scent of blood and spilled coffee filled the air.

Cops rushed inside, followed by EMTs.

Erik raised his hands at his sides as he searched the room.

Where was Korzakov? Erik's heart jumped into his throat. Had the man escaped again? He studied the bodies on the floor.

There.

A man in a beige suit lay half on top of Nicki, a look of shock on his face. A gaping hole in his neck and his left eye a blown-out mess.

Erik barreled forward and shoved Korzakov's dead body aside.

A bloom of red had turned to black on Nicki's chest.

Just like his mother, her hair covered her face.

Her body unmoving.

So very still.

With a deep moan torn from someplace deep inside his soul, he dropped to his knees and cradled Nicki in his arms.

Tears fell unheeded down his cheeks.

Until…a slight puff of air burst upon his neck. "Nicki, can you hear me?" He glanced down at her face then shook her a little.

No response.

"I'm so sorry." He held her in his arms and murmured his apology over and over until the medics came and took her away.

Watching the ambulance leave, he studied the blood on his hands.

Nicki's blood.

Once again, he'd been unable to move as the woman he loved was shot.

But this time, he couldn't seek revenge, because the person responsible lay dead at his feet.

Was that the game life played? Once he'd reached his goal of Korzakov's death, he lost another person in exchange? He rubbed a hand against his breastbone. If Nicki died, where would his desire for vengeance lead him then? Only one answer came. The only person deserving of his hate, his wrath, and his contempt was himself.

His existence was the single reason Nicki and his mother had ended up lying in a pool of their own blood, and because of that he'd walk away from it all and never look back.

CHAPTER TWENTY-SEVEN

Three days after the shooting, Nicki tugged at a loose string on her hospital gown. "You don't have to justify Erik's actions again, Rachel. I know who he is."

Rachel paced beside her bed. "So do I."

"I need to start over, you know? And I can finally do that. It'll be okay."

"I can't convince you to stay here and let me help you?"

"No. I think I'll take a week to just lounge around, and then I have to get back to work. I've been sending out resumes, and I finally got a nice bite from a place down in Cocoa Beach, Florida."

"It's hot as hell down there, Nicki. Not to mention the hurricanes."

"The lady I spoke to seemed really cool. She even said she could hook me up with a place to stay for a while."

"I hate to see you go."

Nicki nodded, and though she tried to feel something, anything, she couldn't. Yet, she knew, at some point, the reservoirs of pain currently stored deep in her heart would burst and she'd lose her shit. She would need to be alone in that moment, because it'd be ugly and hard, and she might not survive. Her heart hurt about as much as the wound in her shoulder. According to Raul, Leonard's shot had derailed Korzakov's and basically kept the bullet from hitting her square in the chest.

"I could just strangle Erik." Rachel roared once again.

Nicki didn't answer. She had put Erik on her mental no-go list. He hadn't visited since she'd been in the hospital recovering from the gunshot wound. Nicki swallowed hard, staving off tears. After the month she'd had, meeting with mafia leaders, shooting a man, being abducted, and getting shot, no one could blame her for being a wreck. Yet, hadn't she fallen in love during that time, too? So, where was her happy ending? Why hadn't love conquered all? Nope. Stop it. Figuring out Erik was beyond her, and she refused to keep contemplating the why's of life.

Instead she would volunteer with local organizations that helped trafficked and drug-addicted girls. That would be her focus in Florida, along with living a quiet and calm life. She sighed and glanced at Rachel. "Your constant care during this time has meant so much. But please, could we not talk about Erik? I have to move past that."

"He's an idiot."

"We'd established that long before now." She smiled, but it was weak, because his abandonment hurt. A lot. How could he walk away after they'd declared their love for each other? "Rachel?"

"Yeah." Her friend turned from staring out the window.

"Will you take my hand?"

"Sure, honey. What's wrong?" Rachel immediately crossed the room.

Nicki gripped her friend's hand, welcoming the warmth. "Do you think everything's really over? Do you think I'm safe?" She couldn't shake the fear that Korzakov could still get to her somehow. Every time she closed her eyes, she saw Erik's body, bloody and beaten. She still felt her helplessness as she'd been dragged before Korzakov. Still remembered the jerk of her body as the bullet fired through her shoulder. Blinking away the memories, she shivered. "Is it cold in here? I'm so cold, and I've got this lump in my throat which blocks my breath." She swallowed hard. "How much more am I supposed to endure? I don't know, but it seems as if I'm getting the shit end of the stick."

Rachel bent and kissed her forehead. "You are one of the strongest women I know...besides me." She grinned. "As far as Korzakov, yes, I believe his reign is over. He's dead. His crew was basically annihilated at the diner."

"I'll never feel safe though. I just won't."

"I understand that, but instead of focusing on your fear, why don't you focus on something more positive?"

"I'm sorry, Rachel, but I'm not seeing the rainbow over this shit storm right now." Think positive? *That* was her friend's advice?

"Hey, storms pass." Rachel touched Nicki's cheek.

Nicki's throat went tight, and she bit her lower lip. "I have a lot to think about. I can't even begin to express how I feel."

"I know what it's like to hold pain inside for too long. That negativity shapes you and holds you down."

"My past will never be fully gone." Nicki wiped a tear from her cheek. "The things I did."

Rachel climbed into the bed beside her and rested her head on Nicki's good shoulder. "How about we try?"

Nicki scooted closer to Rachel's warmth. "Guilt for you and shame for me?"

"Yes."

Nicki took a deep breath then released it, fighting off the urge to cry. "I will try if you will."

"Promise?"

"Yes, but we should pinky shake on it." Nicki held out her little finger.

"Sure, then I think I want to cry a little."

Nicki nodded because she was already crying. *Damn it!*

They wrapped their pinky fingers around each other's, and a little of that pressure in Nicki's heart eased.

Rachel made a pained sound then pressed her face against Nicki's neck and sobbed.

Tears poured down Nicki's cheeks too, and she let them fall all while running her hand through Rachel's thick hair and whispering words of comfort as much for herself as for her friend. She still had a long way to go in order to fully heal, but in this moment, she finally had the will to try.

CHAPTER TWENTY-EIGHT

The seventh day. Wasn't that supposed to be a day of rest...or something? And yet, Erik had never been so unsettled or nervous in his life. Unable to eat, to sleep, to do anything but wallow in a misery of his own making, until he'd had an epiphany.

He loved Nicki, so what the hell was he doing? He didn't back down. Didn't run when things were difficult. He maneuvered, finagled, and found a way to win. Nothing was holding him back anymore, so why had he run scared?

After kicking his ass into gear, he hopped in his car and headed to the hospital, roses in hand, ready to drop to his knees and beg forgiveness. During the past few days, he'd been to see Leonard at the hospital a few times. The man was doing well if all his grumbling had anything to say about the matter. While there, he'd checked on Nicki, peeking into her room like a stalker. Sheridan had almost caught him once, but he'd slipped into another room for a moment.

Rachel had called him over and over again, unaware of his covert visits. He hadn't answered, but he had listened to her irate messages. He'd really blown it with both her and Nicki.

He owed Nicki an apology, if nothing else. He'd gotten her

abducted and shot. Yet, this apology was more for himself than for her, and he knew that, admitted that. Plus, the whole visit was just a way to see her again. After he dealt with Nicki, he'd speak to Rachel and try to unruffle her feathers.

In his head, he really did believe that Nicki and his sister both were better off without him, but he'd been given a taste of a better life. A happy life, and he craved it more than he should.

Nicki made him want to be a better man if only to see her smile. Sappy as hell, he owned that, too, but he couldn't live with her thinking he'd abandoned her, even though in a way, he had. He had to let her know he did love her. Perhaps, he could alleviate her pain a little, especially if her heart hurt as much as his own.

Once at the hospital, he knocked on her door and stepped inside.

All conversation stopped.

Then Rachel charged forward. "What in the hell are you doing here? I called you and you think you can just—"

"I hear you." Erik drew the little, angry tornado into his arms. "I hear you today. I heard you yesterday and the day before that. I've always heard you."

She shoved away and stared up at him with narrowed eyes. "Where have you been, you stupid asshole!"

"Rachel." He glanced over at Nicki, who had her hands fisted in her lap. "I came to speak to Nicki."

"She's leaving later today." Rachel glared up at him, her hip cocked out.

"I know."

"Do you?"

"Yes."

Rachel kept his gaze for a moment then punched him in the arm. Hard.

"Ow! What the hell?"

"Fix this." Grumbling under her breath, she waved a hand at Nicki then flounced from the room.

Erik rubbed his arm then stepped forward. Unsure what to do

with the flowers, he placed them next to the others on a side table. "Brought you these. Should keep for a few days."

Nicki nodded.

Her long dark hair was up in a ponytail. Her face pale. She lay a bit tilted, resting on her non-injured side. Her vibrancy diluted by the white sheets and the haze of antiseptic scent lingering in the air.

"How are you feeling?" *Small talk, always a brilliant idea, Pavel.*

"I'm fine."

"Heading home today?"

"Really, this is what we're doing? Chit chat?" She half-laughed then shook her head. "How about we just get this over with? You *said* you loved me."

Erik rocked back on his heels, stuffing his hands in his front pockets. "I did." He cleared his throat. "I do."

Luckily, they were alone in the room. He'd changed her room to private after making a few phone calls.

She wet her lips then met his gaze. "I believed in you for so long. Even after your harsh words, I still had faith. I knew you could be a good man, because I'd seen that side of you emerge so many times. We were connected you and I. We're the same in so many ways and we understand each other. At least I thought we did...but then...after I'd shot a man, after I'd been abducted by a disgusting pedophile, after I'd been shot, you were nowhere to be found."

Ouch! Her words were deserved, were raw, and he could do nothing to change what he'd done, except to give her a small glimpse of his remorse. "I *was* here."

"Don't you dare!" She straightened, jabbing a finger in his direction.

He stepped closer to the bed. "I came to check on you every day."

"No, you didn't because I didn't *see* you. I didn't hold your hand. I didn't cry on your shoulder, and I sure as hell didn't find comfort in your arms when I had nightmares. I can't rely on you. I can't trust you, and because of that I don't know that I can love you."

"Oh, Nicki, please don't say that." Taking the final two steps, he landed at her side and took her cool hand. "I'm sorry."

"Why?" She glanced at him then turned her attention to their joined hands. She pressed down on his thumbnail. "Why care today when you didn't yesterday?"

"All right." With his free hand, he caressed her cheek. "I deserve everything you've said, but—"

"You don't get a but, Pavel." She jerked her hand away. Her tone was barely above a whisper when she spoke again. "You broke my heart, and I don't want you here."

"I made a mistake and I'll fix it." He brushed a hand across her hair spilling out of the ponytail. "I don't know how to do...relationships."

"Not really that hard." She fiddled with the edge of the pillow-case. "You just have to show up."

"I'm here now." She didn't respond, so he stroked her face again. Her skin almost icy. "Are you cold? Do you need a blanket?"

Nicki huffed out a sigh. "Listen, I have a lot going on right now, I can't take on you and all your issues. Plus, I'm leaving soon and I don't want you and all your mafia drama in my life."

"Well, that's going to be a problem."

"Not on my end."

"You should know me well enough by now to understand that when I want something, I get it. And when I love a woman, I'll do anything for her."

"I thought I did know you, but you proved I didn't."

"And I already apologized for that." He lowered the bed rail and sat beside her.

"Oh right, let's just move on then." She whipped a hand through the air. "You apologized. Everything's perfect now."

"For two weeks it was, and it will be again."

"You listen to me, Erik Pavel." Wincing, she rose up on an elbow. "Not everything is about *you*. Not everything works according to *your* schedule. When and *if* I ever want to speak to you again, I'll let you know."

There was *his* Nicki. He'd worried that her fire had gone out. Needing to stoke the flame, he bent and kissed her. She tasted of coffee and everything he missed. She tasted like love and comfort and home.

Light presses of his lips against hers, trying to warm her, as well as remind her of everything that could exist between them. This fire only burned with her, and while true, he'd taken a while to see the truth, his future was very clear. Nicki Nobles was that future. He eased back, placing a soft kiss on her cheek, her forehead, and once more on her lips. "I love you, Nicki, and I'm so very sorry for what you've gone through because of me. Help me be better. Teach me to do this relationship the right way. I thought I could stay away from you, but turns out I can't." He shrugged, took a deep breath, and then asked the most important question of his life. "Can you forgive me?"

She turned away, tears rolling down her cheeks. "I want to. I really do, but I waited for you every day, and every day ended without you here. Everything hurt, and I was scared, and all I wanted was for you to hold me. I cried. I prayed, but nothing happened. And then today...here you are. A week too late, and I have no idea what to do with you. I'm so angry right now. All I want to do is hurt you as much as you've hurt me. But that's not who I am, so I need you to go until I can decide what *I* want."

"I came today, and I—"

Nicki pressed a finger against his lips. "You did, and I thank you for that, but that's all I have to give you right now."

CHAPTER TWENTY-NINE

After waiting for the pop-up thunderstorm to pass, Erik stepped into the steamy, practically sizzling air in Surfside, Florida. His driver pulled up to the curb, and Erik settled into the sedan's backseat. Sweat trickled down his back. Wearing a suit jacket in this humidity wasn't such a good idea.

He'd spent the last month wrapping up business with Marshal Leonard Moore on the legal side, and Frankie Castillo on the other, all while forging a new position as a consultant against white-collar crime. He had Leonard and his criminal past to thank for this current position.

For the past couple weeks, he'd lived in The Four Seasons Hotel. He leaned back in his seat and checked his texts as the driver weaved through traffic.

The ache in Erik's chest hadn't left since he'd walked away from Nicki, and he hadn't slept much at all. Too much guilt. Too many words left unsaid.

The car came to a stop in a strip mall's parking lot about four miles from his hotel. He had a waxing appointment under a fake name at Nicki's new salon.

He knew where she lived. Had run background checks on each of her roommates. And he knew she hadn't dated anyone since leaving the hospital, but maybe that had to do with her recovery more than anything else.

Last week, Sheridan, Clayton, and Jenny had flown down to Florida—and into his life. He'd actually enjoyed their visit even if they hadn't been invited. Jenny was a whirlwind. She would breeze into a room then hug him, kiss him, and thank him over and over again for saving her life. He smiled and hugged her back, but truly believed Raul and Nicki were more deserving of her gratitude.

A few days into Clayton and Sheridan's visit, Clayton had developed the stomach flu. Erik and Sheridan had gone to the drug store a few times, causing a firestorm of tabloid speculation after they'd been photographed together. He'd laughed at how quickly her life could be misconstrued, which made him ponder his own life.

How many pictures had been forced into his mind on how life was supposed to be? Couldn't he change what people saw just by doing something different, and would that, in turn, change how he saw himself?

Time to find out. He opened the salon's door and stepped inside. The cool air from the air conditioning hit his face. Perhaps the West Coast would be a better place to set up shop, because Florida's humidity was killing him.

Nervous as hell, he checked in with the receptionist and took a seat in an uncomfortable white plastic chair with a pink cushion. He finally gave up trying to get situated; stood, and perused the shelves of hair care products.

He heard her laugh before he saw her, and he turned toward the sound.

Nicki came out of a room in the back, her hair a little shorter, her cheekbones a little sharper. She'd lost weight and didn't have much to lose as it was.

She smiled at her customer and led her to the counter.

Then she saw him.

Her smile dropped, and she narrowed her eyes. After a tense moment, she said, "I assume you're John Wick."

"Yep." He bit back a grin.

"That's not even funny or clever."

"I kinda thought it was." He tugged on the end of his tie. "I mean John Wick *is* pretty awesome."

Nicki braced both hands on her hips. "He's a fictional movie character and besides, who ever said you should think...about anything?"

This was likely true, but at least she was speaking to him. "I'm here for my appointment."

"No, *John Wick* is here. I don't know who you are." She jabbed a finger at him then winced and pressed a hand against her shoulder.

"Damn it, Nicki." He went to her immediately and led her to her room.

"Do not act like you care." She huffed out. "It's your fault I moved too quickly."

"I'm sorry."

"Yeah, well take your sorry and shove it up your ass."

He settled her into a white wicker chair with a floral cushion and then closed the door. "I *am* sorry, Nicki."

"Shut up." She stood and grabbed a water bottle from the tiny fridge that hummed in the corner. Then she went to her appointment book and tapped her finger against the paper. "All right then, John Wick. It says here you want a wax."

God it was good to see her, and her attitude already had him half-hard. Not to mention her tight dark jeans, and that black top that dipped perfectly into a V at her breasts. "I just asked the girl what your longest procedure was, and she said a full body wax so that's what I picked. I don't want a wax, I only wanted to—"

Nicki held up a hand. "Don't want to hear it. You scheduled a wax, so strip and get on the table. *You* decided to take up a block of my time so you' re doing this and you're paying for it. Get naked, Wick."

He held up a finger and shook it back and forth. "I manscape, so I'm all good."

"Nope. Get on the table or leave."

Oh, hell this was going to hurt...a lot.

OUT OF ALL THE dreams Nicki had ever had, and the few great moments of her life, never would she have imagined something as perfect as this.

A full jar of wax.

A freshly opened box of paper strips.

And Erik Pavel's balls on her table.

She closed her eyes and gave thanks to whoever had bestowed her such a gift.

He'd left her alone in that hospital.

And he'd pay.

With her clients, she took great care to be extra-gentle around such sensitive areas, but with this man, all bets were off. She grabbed the scissors and held them up, examining them. Erik had undressed as she'd asked. His gloriously naked form was on her table to do with as she wished, and her traitorous body had a lot of wishes.

"Well, well, well...I find it very interesting that after a month, you deign to visit me. After so much time has passed, I can't imagine what you'd want." She put the scissors back down and picked up her electric clippers.

"Nicki, I—"

She turned on the clippers, blocking his response, because nothing he could say would erase his heartless actions. "Sorry, can't hear you. Working." Pressing a hand against his thigh, she held him still while shaving a swath through his pubic hair, trimming it down so it'd be easier to wax. Though, as he'd said, he was quite clean cut already. She narrowed her eyes, because who the hell did he have to look so pretty for?

Once finished, he started to speak again so she turned the trimmer back on and proceeded to trim his happy trail and his chest. Anger was starting to replace shock at his bold appearance. Just what the hell was he doing here? She stole a glance at her wax pot. Erik Pavel knew all about revenge, and now so would she.

He tried to sit up.

She slammed him back down.

"You don't need to do this. I'll pay for the appointment."

"Oh, you'll pay." She flashed a fake grin.

"Nicki, wouldn't it make more sense to just talk this out?"

"Yes, actually, you're right it would. Perhaps if you'd done so, oh, I don't know, maybe a month or so ago when I was lying in a hospital bed with gunshot wound in my shoulder, I'd have been willing to indulge you."

"I did visit and I am sorry."

"Sorry doesn't mean a whole lot. Sorry is just a word when what I needed was you by my side. I needed you, and you just waltzed in at the end, saying this and that...and...well, where have you been since?" Her throat tightened and her voice started to shake. She took a moment, grabbed her water bottle and downed a big swig. "I've lived through pain and abandonment before, and I will again." She slammed down the bottle, causing a little to splash out the top. "Now, spread your legs a little wider. I'm not going to lie, this'll hurt."

She should just kick him out. But he'd made this appointment, and she had a lot of built up anger, so not only were they doing this, she was going to revel in raining down the pain on Mr. Show-up-out-of-the-blue-for-a-second-time.

Sure, she'd asked for time and space, but when had he ever listened to her before? And now a month later, he just showed up. Her heart might be doing a jig, but her mind still had do-not-pass-go-signs. She grabbed an antiseptic wipe and wiped him down.

He hissed.

"Sorry, I only use *warm* wipes on clients who aren't complete assholes."

"Nicki, I realize you need to get a little of your own back, so go ahead, do your worst."

"*You* are the one who came to *my* job. *You* are the one who scheduled a wax, so I don't know what you're talking about. I'm doing my job. It's as simple as that. So shut up and enjoy. I know I will." After dipping her stick in the hot wax, she didn't blow on it to cool it off before starting with the area between his belly button and pubic hairline. Once she'd laid down a line of wax, she pressed down on a wax paper strip, circled her fingers over it, and then yanked it free.

He yelped and shot straight up.

"Lie back down."

"Holy Jesus!" He narrowed his eyes. "Was that enough payback?"

"Not even close. Lie down, Pavel." She spread wax on the crease of his thigh, pressed down the paper, and yanked again.

He roared out a few choice cuss words. "Are we done now?"

"No." She pressed him back down, fighting a grin. "You'd be uneven."

"Nicki."

Biting her lip to keep from laughing, she ignored his warning tone and waxed his other side.

This time when he shot up, he gripped her shoulders. "That's enough."

Oh no, he did not just put his hands on me. "No, your pain isn't enough." She shoved at his chest. "It'll never be enough! You hurt me! We did the whole declaring our love before we died thing, and you promised me bacon! But then, when I needed you the most, you just walked away. Twice! I don't know if you're aware of this or not, but love means fighting, love means staying and trusting."

"You're right about everything, but you said you needed space, so I—"

"Do not tell me what I said. I know what I said." She paced beside the bed, knowing she came off sounding like a complete idiot. "It's been a month. I never said I needed a month."

"I don't know how long you need. I had a few things of my own to settle too, you know."

"Oh, of course. We're all on your schedule. I forgot. Everything is set according to the master plotter, Erik Pavel. When he's ready, we all jump to attention."

"I would say he's ready." He smirked and waved a hand at his erect dick.

"Oh, you want me to wax your dick? Fine." She pushed him down. "I need to put on gloves first. No telling where that cock has been."

He chuckled. "Go ahead. I promise it's clean. Wax my balls if you need to. Whatever it takes."

She rolled her eyes and sniffed. "I'm kind of over it now. Put your junk away, I'm tired of seeing it."

He gripped his dick. "We've missed you."

Jaw dropping at his audacity, she punched his stomach. "Are you insane?"

"Ow!" He brought up his knees and laid on his side. "What the hell, Nicki?"

"You're lucky I didn't punch your dick, because that's what you deserve. You come in here and apologize and throw out stupid innu-endoes and I'm supposed to do what? Be charmed by you? Forgive you? Why are you here?"

Wincing, he sat up, his legs dangling off her table and his dick hitting his stomach, leaving a smear of pre-cum behind. "Let's back-track for just a moment. A little over a month ago, I took you to a restaurant, like a normal guy would, but our night ended in a flurry of bullets. Not only that, I held you in my arms, thinking you were dead."

"A part of me did die, but that wasn't because of the bullet." She wiped at the tear on her cheek.

"Don't say that, please." He reached out, took her hand, and kissed it. "When I said I loved you, I meant it."

"I'm fine without you, so go away." He couldn't do this. Couldn't come here and be all naked and gorgeous with sadness in his eyes. She'd moved on with her life. But she'd also secretly hoped this moment would come, because she missed him.

"I'll never forgive myself for not being there when you needed me. I know you're fine on your own. I know it'll take a long time to earn your trust, but I do love you, Nicki, and I'm sorry. You can send me away. I deserve that, too. I'll even let you finish waxing my balls and my ass if it'll make you feel better." He settled back on her table, cushioning his head with his arms.

"Fine." She dipped another stick in the wax, shoved his thighs apart, and touched the warmth against his taint. After spreading a small amount, she pressed on a wax strip and pulled it free.

He yelped.

"Tell me why?"

"Why what?" After practically shouting the words, he cupped a hand over his balls and shot her a glare.

"Why did you leave? Why did you come back? How could you do that to me, Erik? I thought you said you would try and then, you didn't. So why?"

He straightened and ran both hands along the tops of his thighs. "I thought you'd suffered enough because of me. And after Korzakov died, I needed to figure out my next steps. I needed time, too, Nicki."

"Of course you did." Nicki gathered up all the used wax sticks and dropped them in the trash. "We're done here."

"Nicki, please."

"You can pay at the reception desk." Suddenly very weary, Nicki ran a hand through her hair. Why did life have to hurt so much? "I'd like you to leave."

"No." He took her hand. "My whole life was about revenge. About taking back a moment in my life when I had no control, but that whole time, I was letting the very thing I hated the most control me. You were right about so many things. You've always been so much stronger than me, so much more compassionate and kind. Your heart is a very precious thing, and I'm sorry I hurt it." He grabbed her hips and drew her between his legs. "You're a fighter. You rise above everything and come out just fine on the other side. You're beautiful in every way, and I don't deserve you."

She scoffed and took a step back. "This is true." He still smelled the same, like lavender and lies, but a part of her wanted to believe him.

He squeezed her hand. "I want to deserve you, Nicki. We found a bit of peace together, didn't we? I still feel like you'll never be safe with someone like me. Yet, that doesn't seem to stop me from wanting you. I'm here and I want to stay."

Nicki swallowed the lump in her throat. "You hurt me."

"I did."

"You're stupid."

"I am."

"I don't really need you."

"I know that, but I need you."

She nodded, not really even sure what she was agreeing to, but her heart knew. That organ was a romantic bitch. "I've been seeing a therapist, and we're working on moving forward. I don't really need her to tell me that, because honestly that's all I've ever done, but I don't know, she's helping."

"That's good, Nicki. I'm proud of you."

She met his gaze and narrowed her eyes. "Don't patronize me, Pavel."

"I'm not. I just said you were stronger than me. No way would I ever lay out my life for someone to analyze."

"Well, out of everyone I know, you need therapy the most."

"I do."

"God, stop being so agreeable."

He held up a hand. "All right. Listen, I'll let you get back to work. Thanks for letting me—"

"Gah! Will you shut up already?" She sighed and rubbed her temples. "There's a simple solution to this entire thing."

"Is there?"

"Yes, something everyone knows." She let a smile slip through, cursing herself for her stupidity, because she shouldn't do this again. Shouldn't take a chance. But she loved him, and when you loved people you forgave them. Although, maybe she should wax his balls just to make sure he knew the height of his transgressions.

"And what is this simple solution?" He tugged on her shirt.

"Kiss it and make it better."

His eyes widened. "That's all I have to do?"

She shrugged. "For now."

And so he did.

And maybe him being naked led to her being naked.

And maybe he kissed the scar on her shoulder, and she finally felt like she could heal.

And maybe, just maybe they had to use a whole lot of sanitary wipes afterwards to clean up her massage bed.

But no maybes this time, the feel of his arms around her, was definitely worth the wait. And if they happened to get wax in unmentionable places, well...that was okay, because *they* were okay. They'd taken something that wouldn't end and made it a new beginning.

EPILOGUE

Erik walked along the beach with Rachel at his side.

"It's nice here." She stopped and stared out at the water.

The waves crashed against the shore, and seagulls flew overhead before diving into the water. He found comfort in the familiar whooshing sound as he considered what to say to his sister. He'd taken this walk with a purpose, yet didn't know how to begin.

"Yeah." He cleared his throat. "We, ah...we like it here. Something about the ocean...I don't know...I find the sounds soothing. I work from home a lot, but have to go into the city sometimes, too."

Three months after the wax-episode, he and Nicki had finally settled in Miami. She worked at a new salon, and he helped investigators around the globe with cases while keeping his toe in investments.

Rachel and Bronco were visiting for a few days over Thanksgiving.

And though Erik had a lot of regrets in his life, he'd also discovered he had a lot to be thankful for too. He and Nicki were still working on trust and building their own form of a relationship. Right now they basically had sex non-stop, which worked for him.

When they weren't in bed, they volunteered at the local women's shelter, and he'd even sat with Nicki a few times during trips to her therapist. Apparently, the woman had her own ideas about how he needed to treat Nicki. He'd listened, but he already knew he needed to be Nicki's friend and lover. Simple in so many ways. Things were so smooth between them, he wondered why he'd fought it at all. Plus all the sex. Yeah, the sex. Nothing remained between them anymore. No past ghosts were allowed in their bed. They had agreed to move forward and just live.

They were happy and everything was finally settling in his life, except for one thing.

Rachel. So much had passed between them. He'd been very cruel. He'd pushed and pushed, and yet, here she was by his side. How could he express what that really meant to him? What *she* meant?

He wanted his sister in his life, and even though Nicki had said he didn't have to say it as much as to live it, he still felt he owed Rachel more. She needed to hear the words, and he wanted to give them to her.

They were alone now, so he'd take this moment to say what he should've said all along. He turned to her and took a deep breath before blurting, "Rachel, would you sit with me for a moment? Sit, here on the beach...with me?"

"Sure." Brow arching, she sank beside him.

After sitting at her side, he remained quiet for a moment, running his fingers through the sand. "I'm sorry for so many things, Rachel."

"I am, too."

"I don't blame you." He wrapped an arm around her tiny shoulders and drew her close.

"Thank you for saying that." She smiled. "I'm happy that you're finally happy. You deserve to be."

"I'm not a good person, Rachel."

"I know." She squeezed his hand on her shoulder.

They stared out at the waves for a while. The warmth of the November day, fading as the sun went down.

Erik ran his fingers through the sand again. "The waves, they just keep rolling against the shore, don't they?"

"It's nice to know they'll never stop." She linked her hand with his and dropped her head on his shoulder.

"It is. You can come here and sit with me any time you'd like, you know?"

"I can?"

"Yeah, you're my sister." He swallowed the lump in his throat. "You're my family, and I like having you here."

He heard a gasp then all of a sudden, Rachel jumped him, knocking him back onto the beach.

She cried against his chest, and he had to wipe tears from his own eyes, but eventually she quieted, and he held her hand as they walked back to the house.

AFTER A ROUND OF HOT, sweaty sex, Erik sucked in air while pressed against Nicki's side. "Jesus, woman, you're going to kill me."

Nicki chuckled, rose above him, and lowered for a long, thorough kiss. "I think we should make this official."

He tensed. "What?"

She kissed him again. "The right answer was, Yes Nicki, let's make this official."

"Official, like marriage?"

"Sure, why not? All our friends are doing it. Let's be cool too."

He scoffed, because what in the hell were they even talking about? "I don't need a piece of paper to tell me that I love you."

"Awe." Nicki kissed his cheek. "That's sweet."

"Plus, fuck me, Nicki, couldn't you let *me* ask *you*?"

"Fine, go ahead."

"I will."

"No, I meant right now."

He slapped her ass. "Bossy little thing, aren't you?"

"You didn't mind it when I ordered you to fuck me harder."

His cock started to swell, and he ran a hand down the smooth skin of her spine. "I think I need to hear that again."

She arched a brow. "Can you?"

He gripped his swollen cock. "It heard you say fuck. My dick doesn't know you were only using the word in conversation."

"Hmmm..." She plopped down at his side, but set her thigh on his waist. "Do you think we'll ever get married?" She twirled a finger through his chest hair.

"Yes, I do."

"Kids?"

"We've got two redheaded sisters that visit, and Sheridan's little boy. I think that's good for now."

"Yeah. I kind of like just you and me."

He took her teasing hand and brought it to his lips. "Just you and me."

She propped her elbow against the bed and rested her chin in her open palm. "Things go well with Rachel earlier?"

"Yeah."

"Good, her eyes were all red when she came back inside, and I worried."

"No, things are good there."

"I'm glad."

"Yeah, me too." Erik closed his eyes but couldn't sleep, plus he was still half-hard.

Life was moving so fast, and he just wanted to take a moment to reflect on it all. They'd have a big Thanksgiving dinner later today, but right now, he needed this quiet moment with Nicki. "Come watch the sunrise with me."

"I'm still in a sex coma."

"Come on." He tugged her from the bed, and they slipped on the barest of clothes.

Barefoot, they walked along the beach.

Erik listened to the crashing waves and breathed in the salty, fresh air. And when the sun burst over the horizon, he held Nicki in his arms. "I want to give thanks...for you. You stuck by me, believed in me, and changed me in ways I'm just beginning to appreciate. Thank you for that."

She turned in his arms and kissed him. "You had to end one life to begin another."

"I did, and I'll be forever grateful I'm starting over with you."

Nicki nodded. "You know what we need to make this moment complete?"

He bumped her with his hips. "I have a few ideas."

"No. That's not it at all." Her tone turned serious. "Erik, listen, I just realized something we've missed along the way."

His brow furrowed. "What is it?"

"I can't believe you forgot." She buried her head in his chest. "I never really got over this void in our relationship."

Heart racing, he ran a hand through her hair. "What is it?"

She leaned back and smiled, then smacked him on the ass. "Bacon. You owe me bacon."

"Damn it, woman you scared me to death."

She laughed then jumped away. "Ha, ha, you fell for it."

"I pour my heart out and all you want is bacon?"

"They're strips of salty goodness."

"I've got a strip of salty goodness for you." Wagging his brows, he lunged for her.

She squealed and sidestepped before running up to the house.

He followed at a slower pace, and once again, thanked whoever was listening that the beautiful creature, currently barging into their house, was capable of making him wish for more than an end.

And with the tiny blue box he had waiting in his drawer, he knew they'd have one hell of a beginning.

Thank you for reading Erik's End. I hope you enjoyed Erik and Nicki's story. If you did, please leave a review at your purchase site. The author appreciates reviews.

Interested in more books in the O-Line series? Visit:
    www.jillianjacobs.com

Please continue for an excerpt from Jillian's paranormal, *Water's Threshold* Book #1 in the Elementals Series.

WATER'S THRESHOLD EXCERPT

*Please enjoy the following excerpt from **Water's Threshold**, Book #1 in **The Elemental Series**. Jillian's Paranormal with Suspenseful Elements.*

Terran Forrester turned up the radio and cracked open the driver's side window, hoping the cold mountain air flowing down from the Tetons would revive him. Driving home this late was not one of his more brilliant decisions. Where his headlights lit the empty road, he scanned for skittering wildlife.

Deer dash is not my game of choice at 2 am.

He would already be home if he hadn't left the National Park Service fundraiser halfway through the evening. As a department head at The Conservancy, his presence was required, although he'd have preferred to skip the affair all together. Black tie events were not his style. A lab coat was his suit of choice.

Talking with Dr. Melinda Givens had offered an escape from stale golf course discussions and details of who had joined who on the

Grand Teton ski slopes this past season. He followed her back to her place for coffee, where she informed him "coffee" was code for kitchen sex. Message received, he stayed for round two in the bedroom. Melinda hadn't expected anything more and that suited him fine. She drifted to sleep with a satisfied smile. So, he threw on his T-shirt, dress pants, and shrugged on his dress shirt before heading out the door. At some point, he would connect with a woman who shared his passion for studying ways to conserve earth's natural resources, but for now, sex fulfilled a basic need, just like food or water.

As the gas needle tipped toward E, he realized his truck also had basic needs. Terran pulled into the only station still lit up on the outskirts of Morgan Junction. Dust stirred as he drove across the gravel lot. While paying for gas inside, he'd grab an apple. The natural sugars would generate a much-needed energy jolt.

After filling the gas tank, he stepped through the automatic doors. A nicely framed young lady, most likely in her mid-twenties, sat at a table by the window. Her long, jean-clad legs were propped against the table's edge as she tipped back in her chair. Her bare toes twitched and her hooded head bopped, no doubt due to the ear buds attached to the iPod in her hand.

Why is she out at this time of night? Why isn't she wearing shoes?

As Terran walked over to the coolers, he spotted a brown minivan pulling up for gas, which sounded a chime at the store's counter. He picked the least-bruised apple from the wicker basket placed inside the cooler and retraced his steps. Stopping next to Shoeless Girl's table, he lightly tapped her shoulder.

She removed one ear bud and raised a brow.

"Excuse me, I'm sorry to bother you. Do you need a ride back to town? Are you waiting for someone?"

She turned away and focused her attention out the window. "No," she answered, and met his gaze in the reflection of the glass. Her sweatshirt hood framed her delicate features and aqua blue eyes.

A tendril of blonde hair escaped from under the hood and shone in bright contrast against the black fabric.

"Kind of late, handsome. Maybe you should hurry home." With a scrape of her chair, she pushed away from the table and exited through the back of the building.

That's what you get for being a nice guy, Forrester.

ABOUT THE AUTHOR

In the spring of 2013, Jillian Jacobs changed her career path and became a romance writer. After reading for years, she figured writing a romance would be quick and easy. Nope! With the guidance of the Indiana Romance Writers of America chapter, she's learned there are many "rules" to writing a proper romance. Being re-schooled has been an interesting journey, and she hopes the best trails are yet to be traveled.

Jillian is a: Tea Guzzler, Polish Pottery Hoarder, and lover of all things Moose.

The genres she writes under are: Paranormal and Contemporary romance with suspenseful elements.

She is the cofounder of Healing With Words, a not-for-profit that hosts Writers On The River.

CONNECT WITH JILLIAN JACOBS ONLINE

Website:
www.jillianjacobs.com

Twitter:
https://twitter.com/GreenMooseProd

Facebook:
https://www.facebook.com/pages/Jillian-Jacobs/737689872920933

Amazon Author Page:
http://bit.ly/JillianJacobsAMZAuthorPage

Goodreads:
https://www.goodreads.com/JillianJacobs